MY DAUGHTER'S BOYFRIEND

DANIEL HURST

www.danielhurstbooks.com

Download My Free Book

If you would like to receive a FREE copy of my psychological thriller 'Just One Second', then you can find the link to the book at my website www.danielhurstbooks.com

PROLOGUE

The missing person poster fluttered in the breeze before taking off completely from the parched desert floor it had been lying on.

It sailed through the air beneath a clear blue sky, the thick red lettering across the top of the poster almost as striking as the red mountains that surrounded this dustbowl several miles outside Los Angeles.

HAVE YOU SEEN THIS WOMAN? the poster asked, just above a photograph of the person in question.

The woman looked to be in her early twenties. She was slender with long dark hair, and appeared to be happy, if the smile in the image was anything to go by. But, of course, the photo had been captured before the woman had gone missing and since nobody knew her whereabouts or what might have happened to her, it was unclear if she was still smiling anymore.

As the poster swirled in the strong breeze, it became caught up in a small dust devil, the name given to a whirlwind that can form in the desert when the hot surface temperature of the dry ground interacts with the cooler air above.

The poster twisted and spun, its edges curling and the image on the poster going in and out of sight quickly before it was spat out and came to a stop on the ground beside a tumbleweed.

As it lay there with the sun beating down on it, the words below the photo were visible.

DESPERATE MOTHER SEEKING ANSWERS – PLEASE HELP ME FIND MY DAUGHTER

Underneath that was a telephone number for anybody who had information about this missing person to call.

But as of yet, nobody had called.

A moment later, the poster was picked up by the wind again and sent onwards into the desert at the mercy of the elements and no sooner had it been taken than a black tarantula crawled across the same spot it had once covered. The arachnid was at home in this brutal environment, which was a lot more than could be said for many of the people who ventured out here, leaving the concrete city behind to experience life in the desert.

While this was a tricky terrain for Americans to navigate, it was even harder for any Europeans who were not used to such barren and brutal landscapes or, indeed, temperatures. It was only an hour after sunrise, but the mercury in the thermometer was quickly rising and would continue to do so for several long hours yet.

Nothing like Europe or, in particular, the UK.

Maybe that was why Dawn Andrews, a mother from the south of England, had wished she'd never come to this place. More than that, she wished her daughter had never come here either.

It had all started with a boyfriend.

Dawn's daughter had fallen in love with an American man.

That was the reason they had come to the United States.

That was also the reason their lives would never be the same again.

BEFORE AMERICA

1

DAWN

It might be summer but that doesn't mean it isn't cold and wet as I make my way through town to meet my friends for our weekly coffee catch-up. Cursing my stupidity at not checking the forecast, I must manage without an umbrella while I begrudge how gloomy the weather in England is during a month that should promise sunshine.

So much for it being June. Instead, it feels like deepest, darkest January as I dodge puddles and pull the zip on my coat a little higher to keep the warmth in. Fortunately, I don't have much further to go, and as I cross the street and push open the door in front of me, I'm relieved to have some respite from the rain.

I'm struck by the strong smell of coffee as I enter the busy café and see a small line of caffeine-hungry customers waiting to get their turn with the skilled barista on the other side of the counter. But rather than join the back of that queue, I make my way over to the large table by the back window, the one that already has three other women sitting at it.

As I get nearer, those three women all notice me approaching and offer a smile and a wave. But it's the drink I'm offered as I take my seat that is of most satisfaction to me because after a late night and a busy morning, I'm eager for the jolt of magic that exists inside the coffee cup now in my hands.

'Thank you,' I say to my three oldest and best friends before I take a sip of my drink because I'm not sure exactly which one of them it was who bought it. But I'm grateful it wasn't me who had to stand in the queue today, although I will have to do so next week in order to return the favour.

'You look like you need it,' says Maggie, the friend I originally made in school but the friend who is still a big part of my life now as each of us negotiates our mid-forties.

'I do,' I confirm, placing my hot cup down on its saucer. 'I'm on night shifts again.'

I'm referring to my job at the 24/7 supermarket where I've worked for the past several years - a job I have never enjoyed, not just because the wages are rubbish, but because there is only so long that stacking shelves can be made interesting before it all just becomes one huge blur of tiring tedium.

'Ahh no, I thought you were done with them?' asks Tanya, another school friend of mine, though we now spend more time talking about our children, our jobs and our monthly household budgets than we do chatting about classroom crushes and playground pranks.

'Yeah, that was the plan. But then, with the increase in energy costs, I had no choice but to ask for more hours. I really need the cash.'

'Tell me about it,' moans Kirsty, my third and final friend at this table who has been in my life ever since our paths crossed at a workplace when we were in our early twenties. Over two decades on and the pair of us are still working just as hard as ever to make ends meet, although my personal circumstances are a little trickier than hers, being that I no longer have a partner who can contribute towards the cost of bills.

'It's crazy how much everything costs these days, isn't it?' Maggie exclaims. 'My electricity bill is through the roof! Then again, it doesn't help when my three boys spend so much time watching TV and playing video games.'

I wince at the thought of how much Maggie's triplets cost her on an annual basis and with that in mind, there is some relief that I only have one hungry mouth to feed.

'Don't worry, they'll be out of your home soon,' Tanya says optimistically but also realistically. 'Are they all still planning on going to uni?'

'Yeah, they are, and I've already told them I can't pay for it all, so they'll need student loans.'

The other women agree with Maggie's decision before they share their experiences with their own children and what life was like when they each left home. Tanya's two daughters did the university thing, too, and are now renting with boyfriends as they start to build their careers in the working world. As for Kirsty, her son left school at sixteen and began working as an electrician, making him self-sufficient very quickly, while her daughter is already in the process of purchasing her first home at the age of twenty-three.

That's the reason I've gone a little quiet now at the table as my three friends continue to chat about the cost of parenting and how things change when the kids grow up and move out.

I'm the only one who is yet to experience what it's like when my child leaves home.

As the mother to a beautiful and bright daughter, Ellie, I'm aware I have absolutely nothing to complain about. But even though that's the case, there is one gripe I have and it's that Ellie is twenty-four, still living under my roof and is showing absolutely no signs of doing anything to change that fact.

It's not that I hate having her around because I don't. If she wasn't still in my house, then I'd be living alone, and that worries me almost as much as the expensive household bills do. But I'm a realist, and not only am I aware she surely can't live with her mother forever, I also wouldn't want her to. I know it will be far healthier for her to strike out on her own and forge her own path in life. Buy her own place. Decorate it to her tastes. Have some privacy. And one day, perhaps, fill that home with a family of her own.

But as yet, Ellie is not going anywhere - a fact not lost on my friends.

'How's Ellie doing?' Maggie asks me before taking a sip of her Americano.

I know that Maggie has only asked because she genuinely cares about me and my daughter and would like to hear an update, but I can't help feeling under pressure as my brain searches for something to tell them. But in the end, and as always, I'm honest with my friends.

'No change there,' I say, trying to make my voice sound light and breezy but not doing a very good job of it. 'She's still working at the restaurant, and she still hates it.'

'She'll find her lane,' Tanya says very kindly, well aware that my daughter still has no idea what she wants to do career-wise so has just been working shifts serving Italian food to hungry diners for the past eighteen months. 'At least she's getting experience, and the tips must be good there, right?'

'I don't know. She never tells me,' I admit. 'She just stays in her room most of the time when she's home. I wonder if she'd ever come out if she didn't have work to go to. She barely sees her friends much anymore either.'

I go to pick up my cup again but glance at Maggie as I do, and I see her grimacing at Tanya and Kirsty, clearly acknowledging that I'm not having the best of times when it comes to my offspring.

'Have you had another go at asking her to contribute to the bills?' Kirsty asks then. 'Or see if she might be willing to pay rent or anything?'

'No, but I know I should do,' I say. 'It's just it was such a disaster last time that I'm scared to broach the subject again.'

Calling it a disaster is an understatement. It was six months ago when I asked Ellie if she could pay something towards her costs of living with me, not wholly because I needed the financial help but because I was trying to teach her that being an adult means having responsibilities. But she just got angry at me, and after telling me how little she makes per hour at the restaurant, she accused me of trying to force her out of the house. That was not the idea - I simply wanted her to know that she couldn't expect to live with me for free forever, and while I knew she didn't have much money, maybe that realisation should have suggested she might try and find a better-paying job so she could earn more. But because our argument got so heated, I have been terrified of having a repeat of that, which is why Ellie is still living at home rent-free and still oblivious to what it's like to have bills to pay each month.

'She'll be okay,' Tanya tells me, putting a reassuring hand on my arm. 'Kids are difficult but girls especially so. They can be very stubborn, but she's still young. I reckon this time next year, she'll have got herself a job she enjoys and be living in her own place with a partner or a friend, and you'll wonder what you were so worried about.'

I smile because I appreciate the optimistic prediction. But beneath the surface, I cannot help but worry that it is well wide of the mark. So far, Ellie has done nothing to suggest that she is looking for a job she likes, nor does she mention any boyfriends or anything like that. But without somebody to split the rent and bills with on whatever place she might move into, I have no idea how she'll ever afford it. That all adds up to her being at home for a long time yet, while all my friends see their children spreading their wings and thriving as they become independent, responsible adults.

'So, does anybody have a holiday booked?' Kirsty asks, switching to a more pleasurable topic. 'I don't know about you girls, but I can't wait to get away from this rain.'

Tanya tells us that she and her partner are thinking of booking a last-minute trip to Italy, a place that sounds delightful and somewhere I'd love to go one day, while Maggie mentions that she is off to Tenerife at the end of the month, although, as always, she's not sure how much of a holiday it will be with triplets in tow.

'What about you, Dawn?' Kirsty asks me as she adds another sachet of sugar to her coffee. 'Going abroad this year?'

I really wish I had something exciting to tell my friends. Perhaps some tale of how I'm whisking myself away to a sun-kissed island for a week or two of rest and recuperation where I will over-indulge in copious amounts of cocktails and Vitamin D. But I can't do that because I have no plans to go abroad this year, or any other year for that matter.

'No, nothing booked yet,' I say, trying to make it sound like there's a chance that might change soon. 'Maybe I'll do something towards the end of summer. There are usually some good deals on then.'

My friends all agree with me, though I can't help but detect a little awkwardness, or even sadness, between them. I know why that is, but I don't bother to acknowledge it. It has nothing to do with me having very little money, that's for sure. Rather, it's more to do with the fact I have nobody to go on holiday with, barring my daughter, who seems to hate me, of course.

As the conversation moves onto yet another topic and my three friends excitedly chat about that new television show that has us all anxiously awaiting the next new episode, I try my best to be happy and enjoy their company. But it's tough, not just because I'm envious of them all with their ambitious children and exciting travel plans but because I'm also jealous of the fact that they have a partner to share everything with at home.

I no longer have that.

All that is waiting for me when I get back to my house later is a moody, stubborn young woman who won't have any interest in talking to me if she can help it.

2

DAWN

My house is quiet as I enter it, but I know I'm not alone. Checking the time, I see that it's only 4 pm, so I still have a few hours until I need to report back to the supermarket for my latest night shift. I also know that Ellie has a couple of hours before she is expected back at the restaurant, not that I expect to see much of her in that time.

As always, she is in her bedroom, the door closed, as sure a sign as any that she does not want company. But I'll be damned if I'm going to go a whole day without seeing the person I share this house with, so without hesitating, I knock on the door before opening it and striding in.

I'm expecting to find Ellie lying in bed watching television, which is how she usually spends the free time she has before going back to work. But this time, she surprises me, and instead of being fixated on the TV, she is instead sitting in front of her laptop.

A laptop that gets closed quickly when she sees that I'm here.

'Mum! What are you doing just barging in?' Ellie cries as I note the closed curtains, dirty plate by the bed and numerous items of clothing littering the floor.

'I didn't barge in,' I clarify. 'I knocked. Didn't you hear me?'

'No, I didn't!'

'Why? What were you doing?'

'None of your business!'

And so it begins again. Another day, another argument.

'It's four o'clock in the afternoon,' I say as I make my way over to the curtains before pulling them open, allowing some much-needed sunlight to enter this room.

'Mum! Leave them shut!' Ellie cries, and suddenly, I'm transported back ten years to when Ellie was a fourteen-year-old who had to be woken up so she could get to school in time. I swear there were some mornings when it would have been easier to raise the dead than it was to raise my own child. The sad thing is, several years on and very little has changed.

'What have I told you about lying in bed all day? You need to get up and do something. It's not healthy to stay in your bedroom all the time.'

'I'm not in here all the time. I'm going to work soon!'

'But this is your free time, Ellie, so don't you want to do something a little more productive with it?'

'What I do in my free time is my business!'

'No, it's my business too because you're living under my roof, in case you hadn't noticed.'

'Urghh, Mum, just get out!'

'No, I will not!'

Yet again, I've managed to become embroiled in another stand-off with my daughter. But while I try to avoid these some days, or at least pacify any argument if it gets going, I'm not in the mood to do that today. After spending the last few hours with my friends and hearing all about the wonderful things their children are doing with their lives, I've had enough of my child wasting hers.

'What's your plan, Ellie?' I ask as I pick up several items of clothing from the floor and put them in a pile on a chair in the corner.

'My plan? What are you talking about? I'm going to work at the restaurant tonight, like always.'

'I don't mean today. I mean long-term. When are you going to get your life in order and become an adult? I'm sick of tidying up after you! You're twenty-five next year, Ellie. Isn't it time you grew up?'

'You mean, isn't it time I moved out? That's what you want, right? You want me gone. Trust me, I want to be gone too, but I don't have any money! How am I supposed to get a place on my own when I make £10 an hour as a waitress?'

'Get another job then! Or ask for more shifts!'

'I don't want to do that!'

'Welcome to the real world! It's not about what you want to do, it's what you have to do!'

I actually hurt my throat with how much I strained my voice then as I shouted at Ellie, and when I notice how shocked she is at my rant, I realise I might have overdone it slightly.

Putting down the latest batch of dirty clothes I'd just picked up, I make my way over to the bed and take a seat on the edge of it.

'I'm sorry,' I say. 'I'm just tired from working all night and then coming home to more jobs to be done.'

'I'm tired too.'

I think about my daughter, who, at just over two decades my junior, can't possibly know the meaning of the word 'tired', but I bite my lip and let that thought pass before continuing.

'I just want you to be happy,' I say, hoping my argumentative child believes me.

'Funny way of showing it.'

'Ellie.'

'No, Mum. Just leave it. I need to get ready for work.'

Ellie clearly wants me to go, and even though we have hardly resolved anything here, I lack the energy to stay in this room any longer.

I head for the door, stepping over other discarded items as I go, but I don't bother to pick anything else up. What's the point? It'll all end up back on the floor again by tomorrow.

I think about offering to make Ellie a cup of tea or a sandwich before she leaves for her shift but decide against it at the last second because maybe that's part of the problem. I do too much for her, make things too easy for her. Why would she ever think about moving out when she has me to run around after her, cooking, cleaning and paying for everything? That's why I just close her bedroom door and go back downstairs, though as I do, I'm sure I hear her start talking to somebody.

Pausing before I'm all the way down, I listen carefully and sure enough, I can hear Ellie's voice. I wonder who it is she is talking to and also wonder how she could so quickly go into a conversation with another person after just having an argument with me. I guess the argument didn't have any impact on her at all. She's just carrying on as normal, chatting to a friend or whoever it might be, presumably over the phone. Or maybe she was talking to somebody on her laptop just before I walked in. She certainly closed the screen down quickly enough, suggesting she didn't want me to see what she was doing.

Was she talking to a boy? Is she in a relationship?

As her mother, it would be nice to know, and I should have a right to know but I don't.

Ellie will tell me if she wants to, but somehow, I have a feeling she doesn't.

I'm utterly despondent as I enter my kitchen and make myself a hot drink, and it's all because I feel like I'm out of my depth and unable to solve the puzzle of my daughter alone. It's times like these a parent needs another person to lean on and ideally, that would be the other parent, the person who takes co-responsibility for the child they brought into the world. But that's not an option for me, and as my eyes land on the photo on the fridge, my heart breaks again, as it does every morning when I wake up and remember the man I lost along the way.

The photo on the fridge, the one inside the Disneyland magnet, shows me as a fresh-faced thirty-year-old, all suntanned and sexy in a crop top and shorts. Standing to my left in the image is Ellie, a cute-as-can-be nine year old with a big smile on her face and a pair of Minnie Mouse ears sitting on top of her head. And on the other side of me is Sean, a ruggedly handsome man with his arm over my shoulder and a big grin on his face, the kind that says he knows how lucky he is to be in Florida with his beautiful family.

He was right. He was lucky. We all were.

But then our luck ran out.

It was seven years after that happy photo was taken when Sean first started to complain of bad headaches, though considering his job on a noisy building site where he worked as a labourer, neither one of us was particularly concerned. But as the headaches worsened, affecting everything from his ability to sleep to his ability to even concentrate during a simple conversation with me, we started to worry that something was seriously wrong.

It took another eighteen months before we got confirmation of that.

Sean had a brain tumour, a shocking diagnosis that caught us both completely off guard. I just thought he was suffering from bad migraines and expected a doctor to eventually find something that would help with them. But it was much worse than that, and as Sean was taken into the hospital to be operated on, I feared the worst for my family.

I couldn't lose him. Neither could Ellie. But what if we did?

How would we cope?

Fortunately, the operation itself was as successful as it could be, and the doctors were confident they had removed most of the tumour. The problem was that they couldn't get it all and that meant that while Sean had been given time, that was all he had. The clock was still ticking and despite me refusing to believe it, we were told that the best-case scenario was that he would last two or three years before operating would have no further effect and his health would deteriorate beyond the point of being able to save him.

My brave, brilliant husband lasted a little longer than the doctor's prognosis, making it almost four years before he slipped away, a fact I know he was proud of because he was as stubborn as me and certainly as stubborn as our daughter and wanted to defy the odds for as long as he could. But he couldn't fight his fate forever, and as he lost his battle, cruelly taken from the world not long after his fortieth birthday, I was suddenly confronted with a terrifying new reality.

Not only was I a heartbroken widow.

I was a single parent on a low income with a teenage daughter who depended on me.

As hard as it has been for me to cope with Sean's loss, I know it has been just as brutal for poor Ellie, who lost her father at an age when all of her friends still got to enjoy having theirs around. I also know that probably some of the reason she has such a lack of motivation and a sense of apathy towards the world is because she is aware how cruel and often pointless life can sometimes be.

Can I really blame her for not wanting to go out to work, earn money, fall in love and buy a home when she has seen her mother do all those things only to end up miserable, stressed and alone anyway?

Sean's death four years ago changed my life forever, though I always accepted it would, which is why

I have had little interest in ever trying to move on with somebody else. But what I find harder to accept is that it has changed Ellie's life too, seemingly stunting her growth before she became a fully grown woman.

As I hear music start to play from my daughter's bedroom upstairs, a sign that tells me she is getting ready for work, I let out a deep sigh. It's a sigh that confirms what I already knew.

Little did this family know it at the time but our lives when that photo in the fridge magnet was taken had peaked then.

That trip to America was as good as it was ever going to get for us.

Everything has been downhill ever since.

3

ELLIE

I turn the music up a little louder before I get back on the bed and pick up my diary. I'm hoping the noise coming from my room will put Mum off from barging in again, though I can't be certain about that because, as she likes to remind me every single day, this is her house and I'm just living in it - as if I could forget that and as if I'd actually stay here if I had any other choice. But who knows - maybe soon, I might just have that choice I so desperately crave.

Opening my diary and finding the first empty page since my last entry, I pick up my pen and start writing.

I spoke to Daryl again today and this time it was a video call!

My lips curl into a smile as I think about the conversation I just had on my laptop with the guy who I am quickly falling in love with.

It was so cool to actually see him live and chat to him properly rather than just over text messages. He looks even hotter than in his photos! I hope he thinks I'm hot too. I put on some make-up for the call but not too much because I remember he said he likes it when girls are confident enough to be natural. I'm definitely not confident enough to wear zero make-up in front of a guy I like, but I don't think he would have noticed that I had a little blusher on.

I also think about how I'm glad Mum didn't notice I had some blusher on either when she stormed in because if she had, then she might have asked why I was wearing make-up when I had been lying in bed all day. But she didn't notice. She only notices the bad stuff, like how untidy my room is or how I am still living here when she wants me gone.

Returning to much more pleasant thoughts, I think about Daryl again, and as my smile returns, my pen moves swiftly across the page.

It was so nice to see him on screen. His bedroom looks cool - much bigger than mine, and he does have a swimming pool, so of course his house is better. Or his dad's house anyway. But at least his dad isn't trying to force him out of his home…

Despite trying my best to forget about Mum and focus on what makes me happy, I can't help but feel frustrated at how she just treated me. Even more than that, I'm frustrated that she walked in as I was talking to Daryl because I had no choice but to slam my laptop shut so she couldn't see what I was doing.

She doesn't know about Daryl and I don't want her to. She'd only criticise me and judge me before telling me what to do, and I bet she'd tell me to stop talking to him. I know she would. She'd say it was stupid that I was talking to a guy in America and that I was wasting my time because we're so far apart. But she doesn't have a clue. It's not a waste of time, even though the distance between us does feel huge.

I like Daryl, and he likes me, and most of all, he makes me happy. Isn't that what Mum wants? She says that, yet she has a funny way of showing it, which is why I will keep this a secret from her.

Daryl looked so cool in his LA Dodgers baseball cap. I wish I had a suntan like him! He says it's hot every day there. I told him what it's like here. How it rains all the time, even in summer. He laughed at that and then he said something amazing. He said that when we finally get together, I'll have to go to him because California is way better than snooze-fest Suffolk.

I break off from writing again as a jolt of excitement runs through my body. It's excitement at the prospect of actually being with Daryl in person and physically being able to touch each other for the first time ever.

Hold hands. Hug. *Kiss.*

So far, all our interactions have been over the internet, which is the only way it could be, considering we live over 5,000 miles and eight time zones apart. Yes, I Googled it.

We first started talking to each other when we randomly matched on a social media site in which users from anywhere in the world are linked into a private conversation with each other. It's a cool app and since I downloaded it six months ago, I've had messaging chats with all sorts of people, from a girl in Argentina to a crazy cat lady in Australia. There have also been a few people from the UK I've spoken to as well, but they were all pretty boring, and a few of the guys who initially seemed interesting turned out to be creeps who wanted photos from me but wouldn't send any of themselves in return. I bet that was because they were much older than they said they were in their bios, probably like forty or something.

Urgh, ancient artefacts.

But then I started messaging Daryl. I could tell that he was different straight away, not just because his bio was full of palm tree and sun emojis, but because of the language he used when we started messaging. He had this ultra-cool, laid-back style to his writing as if it was effortless and he was just saying the first thing that came to his mind. Not like me, who spends hours agonising over every little thing I put into print. I want to be a writer one day, although the only thing I've managed to write so far is my diary, and that is hardly a literary masterpiece.

Going back to the diary, I force myself to write again because not only is that the best way for me to learn my craft, but I've also discovered it's the best way for me to sort out the jumble of thoughts in my head.

It's been that way ever since Dad died.

I'm glad I got to have the video call with Daryl, and I think it was going well before Mum came in. We chatted the whole time, so there were no awkward silences. He made me laugh, and I made him laugh a couple of times too, although maybe he was just laughing at how bad my sense of humour was. But we got on so well, even better than we have in all the messages we've sent over these past few weeks. I wish I was still talking to him now, but I can't risk it with Mum back in the house, so I told Daryl we'd have to do it another time. I also apologised for ending the call so

abruptly, but he seemed to understand. He knows what it's like to not get much privacy.

I break off from writing again as I think about how similar Daryl and I really are. Not only are we the same age, but we both still live at home. But perhaps the biggest similarity, and certainly the one that makes me feel closer to him than any of the others, is that we both know what it's like to have lost a parent.

Daryl's mum passed away three years ago, not long after he had graduated from college. He told me how, after living on campus at a university in Texas from the age of eighteen to twenty-one, he had never planned on moving back home to live with his family permanently again. But his mum died suddenly, a heart attack at home at just forty-three, which is just so tragic, and worried about his dad being alone, he moved back home and has been there ever since.

A tear falls from my eye and hits the open page of my diary, but I don't brush it away, instead watching it sink into the ink and make my writing a little blurry. It's an imperfection of this diary now but that's okay because everything is imperfect. I certainly am and I guess I always will be because I'll never get over what happened to my dad, just like Daryl will never get over what happened to his mum.

Or maybe we will.

Maybe, when we're finally together, things will be easier for the both of us, and we can help each other heal.

The only problem is so many things have to happen first before we can be together.

We have to bridge the massive distance between us, something that will require time, money and one of us venturing into the unknown to see the other.

But that's just the easy part.

The hard part is the first part.

The part where I tell my mum that I have a boyfriend in America.

4

DAWN

My night shift finishes at 4 am, just as the sun is starting to show itself on the horizon. Working at a time when most humans sleep is not easy, nor particularly healthy if the research on circadian rhythms is to be believed. But sometimes I don't have a choice, and while I hate ending my working day just before most people start theirs, I console myself with the knowledge that the extra few hundred pounds this overtime will furnish me with will come in very useful when the next set of bills arrive in the post.

Another benefit to working nights is that as I drive home, the roads are quiet. No rush-hour commute for me. Then again, I still have one big problem facing me. I have to somehow try and get some sleep during the day when the sun is up, the temperature is rising and there is a whole world of noise going on outside my bedroom window.

As I move through the mostly vacant streets and witness an admittedly quite spectacular sunrise over this town, I think about how tired I feel. But it's not just the tiredness from completing an eight-hour shift stacking shelves and completing stock-takes in a supermarket. It's the tiredness that comes from having gone far too many years without any kind of a break.

I've not had a holiday since Sean passed away, choosing instead to throw myself into looking after Ellie and providing the financial support the pair of us need. Sean didn't have life insurance when he got ill, which seems stupid in hindsight, but how many fit and healthy males in their thirties do? Sure, there are some sensible ones who plan ahead but the majority assume they have a long time before they need to worry about their mortality and quite rightly so at that age too. But with Sean leaving very little behind when he passed, I've worked at least five days a week every week ever since to keep my family afloat and that, along with all the grief, anxiety and general stress just from being a busy human in this crazy world, has led to me feeling absolutely exhausted.

I reach my house ten minutes later and park on the driveway before getting out of the car and closing the door behind me as quietly as possible. I'm aware that everyone else on my street will be sleeping now, including the person inside the house I've just parked outside of, so I need to make as little noise as possible. I don't want a repeat of what happened a few months ago when I came back from one particular night shift and, in my sleepy state, somehow managed to accidentally activate the alarm on my car as I was leaving it, ensuring all my neighbours got quite a rude awakening well before their alarm clocks had been due to go off.

Entering my house, I tiptoe through the hallway, removing my coat and shoes as silently as possible before I head for the staircase. I know all the creakiest steps from memory so I avoid those ones for the sake of my sleeping daughter, and as I make it upstairs, I'm relieved to know I'm now only a few yards away from my warm, cosy bed.

I plan on sleeping until midday, before I'll get up, have something to eat and try and have some semblance of a conversation with Ellie before I return to the supermarket to do it all again.

That's my life.

Work. Eat. Argue. Sleep. *Repeat.*

But just before I can go into my bedroom, I notice that Ellie's door is slightly ajar and as I pass it, I can't resist taking a quick peek inside. Despite how disastrously our last interaction went, I still love my daughter and like to know that she is safe, so I'm hoping to see her sleeping soundly underneath her duvet. But I get a surprise when I see the light from her phone screen and as I watch, I see she is typing away on her device.

She's clearly wide awake.

'Hey, is everything okay?' I ask as I open the door a little more and poke my head into her bedroom. When I do, Ellie instantly rolls over and looks surprised to see me.

'What are you doing?' she asks me, annoyed that I've caught her.

'I've just got back. I was going to bed but noticed you were still awake. What's wrong? Can't you sleep?'

'Nothing's wrong,' Ellie grumbles before she rolls back over, turning her back to me once again.

I consider leaving it there but rather than go to bed and try and sleep on yet another bad interaction with my daughter, I venture further into her room.

'Mum, get out,' Ellie groans.

'Relax, I'm not here to have a go at you. I just want to talk,' I say before I hint at wanting to take a seat on the edge of her bed.

For a second, I think that Ellie is going to reject my advances and tell me to leave again but she doesn't. Maybe she's too tired to do that, but I'll take that as a positive for now, and after I sit down beside her, I offer a smile.

'How was work?' I ask her. 'Was the restaurant busy last night?'

'It was alright,' Ellie mumbles back, her phone still in her hand, although the screen is now locked, so I can't see what she might have been doing on it.

'Did you get any good tips?'

'Not really. We have to share them with the chefs anyway. I told you that.'

'I know, I'm just asking.'

'Who cares?'

'I do.'

Ellie rolls her eyes and looks ready for me to leave her alone. But I'm not quite ready to do that yet.

'Why can't you sleep?' I ask her, worried about what the answer might be and fearing it might be for the same reason I can never sleep much these days. It's because the long, dark, lonely nights only make me think of what I've lost, and I worry they might be doing the same for Ellie. I know she hardly slept in the first few years after Sean died but I had hoped she'd gotten over that problem. But if she's still awake in the early hours of the morning, then I guess not.

'I just woke up,' Ellie replies. 'I'm going back to sleep now.'

'I wish I could fall asleep while I was on my phone,' I say, referencing the device she's still holding tightly in her hand. 'What are you looking at on there?'

'Nothing!'

The way Ellie replies so abruptly makes me think she has something to hide. If not, she could have just said she was browsing the internet, and I'd have left it at that.

'Are you messaging somebody?' I ask, but though Ellie shakes her head, the flash on her phone screen a second later gives the game away. She's clearly just received a new message. But from who? Who else could be awake at this time?

'Is it a friend?' I ask, eager to know more about my daughter and her social life, a social life that isn't exactly non-existent but is nowhere near as full as it could be for a twenty-four-year old woman.

'None of your business,' Ellie tells me.

'Why won't you tell me?' I say, keeping my voice calm because I'm not here to pick a fight; I'm just genuinely interested in what might be going on in my child's life, as any other parent would be. Then it occurs to me.

'Do you have a boyfriend?' I ask, wondering if that is the reason my daughter is being even more coy than usual.

'What? No!'

Now she's ultra-defensive, and that makes me think she is lying.

'Ellie, it's okay if you do. You can tell me,' I say, hoping that she will do so if there is a special someone in her life now. I might have lost someone I loved, but it would warm my heart to know my daughter might have met someone who makes her happy.

'Just leave it,' Ellie moans, and she goes to put her phone down on the bedside table on the opposite side of the bed to me so it's well out of my reach. But as she does that, I catch a glimpse of the name on the screen above the message she just received.

'Daryl? That's a nice name,' I say with a smile because now I do know it's a boy. 'Does he work at the restaurant?'

'Mum, just go away!' Ellie groans.

'Why can't you tell me? I don't care if you're seeing someone; it would just be nice to know, that's all.'

'You don't care? Yeah, right! You just want all the details so you can judge us and then probably tell me to stop seeing him.'

'I wouldn't do that!'

'You did it with Andy!'

Ellie has a point there. I did tell her to stop seeing Andy, the last guy she was dating, although there were extenuating circumstances there.

'That was only because he was a complete waste of space,' I say, referring to not only the fact that he couldn't hold down a job, but also that he'd recently got out of prison for aggravated assault. 'He was a criminal.'

'He wasn't a criminal,' Ellie says, her voice dripping in disdain, but even though she is very wrong about that, I don't wish to argue about this, so I just let it go and move on.

'Look, love. I just want you to be happy. As long as Daryl makes you happy, and assuming he's not also an ex-inmate at the local prison, then I'm fine with you seeing him, whoever he is.'

'Really? You just want me to be happy?'

'Yes, of course!'

Ellie seems to think about that fact for a moment before she speaks again.

'Okay, I have a boyfriend,' she admits.

'Great!' I say, genuinely happy because all this time, I just thought my daughter was moping around in her bedroom and hating her life. 'How long have you been seeing him?'

'A while.'

'How did you meet?'

'It's complicated.'

'Try me.'

I smile at Ellie to show her that there is very little that could surprise me, although she puts that to the test a moment later.

'We started messaging online.'

'Oh, okay,' I say, trying to ignore a few alarm bells that are already ringing in my head. But this is the modern age, the world of the internet, so maybe it's not weird. 'How did you two get in touch?'

'There's an app that randomly puts people together into conversations. Most of the time, it's just rubbish, but occasionally, you get chatting to somebody you might get along with.'

'Like a dating app?'

'Not exactly. But I guess it could be.'

'Okay, so what happened? You started messaging Daryl? Where does he live? Is he local?'

'Not exactly.'

'Oh, okay. Does he live far away? Up north, maybe?'

Ellie is very quiet now.

'Ellie? Where does he live?'

'America.'

'What?'

That was not the answer I was expecting and Ellie obviously knows that because she quickly tries to qualify it.

'It's not what you think! We've been talking every day and-'

'-he lives in America? How's that going to work? How can he be your boyfriend if you've never even met?'

'We have met. We had a video call yesterday.'

'A video call is not a meeting! Is that what you were doing when I came in here yesterday and you shut your laptop? You were on a call with him? Who is this guy?'

'He's my age.'

'Is he? How do you know that? What if he's just pretending? It's the internet; anybody can pretend to be anybody on there!'

'Mum, just leave it. I knew you wouldn't understand!'

'Understand? A minute ago, I didn't even know you had a boyfriend, and now you tell me you're dating some guy from America! What do you expect me to think? It's not exactly normal, is it?'

'Get out!'

'No, I want to know exactly who this guy is!'

'Go away!'

Ellie pushes me off her bed then, and even though I wish to find out more about this mysterious man in America who has been having video calls with my daughter, I realise I'm not going to learn much at the moment. Nor is it the best time to because it's still very early and the pair of us are sleep-deprived.

'I'm going to bed,' I say as I head for the door. 'But when I wake up, I want you to tell me all about this new *boyfriend* of yours.'

I make sure to emphasise the boyfriend part of that sentence and maybe I shouldn't have done so, but I wanted to highlight just how ridiculous it is if my daughter thinks she is in a relationship with some guy on the other side of the world, a guy who most probably is not who he says he is.

As I leave Ellie's bedroom and go into mine, I am almost regretting bothering going to speak to her in the first place. But I'm glad I did because at least now I know about this American guy.

That means if something dodgy is going on, I can hopefully put a stop to it before it gets out of hand.

5

DAWN

Despite planning on getting some much-needed rest, I haven't been able to sleep a wink since I got into bed. Another futile glance at my alarm clock tells me that it is now 8 am, and even though I could technically stay in bed all day because my next shift doesn't start for almost twelve hours, I know that it's pointless because I can't drift off. There's too much on my mind, and once again, my daughter is the cause of my worries.

It was surprising, although quite heart-warming at first, to learn that Ellie had a boyfriend, and I did try to make it clear when I first found out that I just wanted her to be happy. I also showed as much of an interest as I could, enquiring about the young man in question to find out how she had met him and where he lived. But that was when things got weird, and after Ellie admitted this particular boyfriend was based in America, I was unable to keep my concern to myself.

Can Ellie blame me for being worried? Who the hell is this guy she met on the internet? Is he who he says he is, or is he some creep, or worse, some criminal trying to take advantage of her? Is he playing on my daughter's emotions for some reason? Will he want her to send him money at some point? Or will he want her to go over and see him only for Ellie to get there and find out he's actually some old guy who plans on locking her in his basement because he's always wanted to take a young British woman as a prisoner?

Okay. I might be getting a little carried away, and I can blame that on my lack of sleep, but even if I was fully rested, I'd still be worried because there's no denying this is unusual.

Why couldn't Ellie have just met a local guy, one who could come over for dinner and I could get to know?

Why did she have to get involved with a guy who lives in another country?

Why does she always have to be different and make things so difficult?

I persist for another fifteen minutes before I give up on sleep completely and get out of bed, putting on my dressing gown and slippers and going downstairs to make some breakfast. I have no idea how I'll get through my next night shift later if I haven't slept, but I'll cross that bridge when I come to it. For now, my only concern is Ellie, and when I hear her moving around in her room, I guess she is just as wide awake as I am.

Ellie joins me in the kitchen a few minutes later, no doubt tempted in by the smell of the toast I'm making, and doing my best to keep things civil between us for as long as possible, I put two slices of bread into the toaster for her before offering her a glass of orange juice.

'Thanks,' she says quietly as she takes a seat at the table, and while I notice that she is on her phone again, possibly messaging Daryl or whoever he really is, I resist the urge to say something and just focus on making breakfast.

'There you go,' I say as I place Ellie's meal down in front of her before taking a seat opposite.

'Thanks.'

'Did you get some sleep?'

'Yeah. You?'

I shake my head.

The pair of us eat our toast in silence for the next couple of minutes, neither one of us seemingly daring to say too much of anything for fear of it ruining the brief ceasefire that currently exists between us. But eventually, I can't resist any longer and tentatively broach the subject of Ellie and her American boy.

'Tell me about him,' I say, silently promising myself that I will say nothing to judge this so-called boyfriend until Ellie has finished whatever she has to say about him.

'He lives in LA,' she begins, and it's obvious from how her face lights up when she says the name of the city that she is already enamoured with the thought of blue skies, palm trees and the Hollywood sign. She might well be too, because she's only seen that part of the world on television before, as have I.

'Okay. You say he's the same age as you?'

'Yep, twenty-four.'

'How did you get talking to him? Who made the first contact?'

'The app just assigns two people into a chat, so it was random. Luck, I guess. Or fate.'

I try not to roll my eyes at Ellie's innocent use of the word 'fate' because while she might believe in romantic fairy tales, I am old enough to know that they rarely occur.

'So what happened? You just started messaging?'

'Yeah, that's how it works. I asked him questions and he asked me a few. It just went from there.'

'When did this start?'

'About six weeks ago.'

'And you message every day?'

'Yeah, pretty much. But yesterday was the first time we'd organised a video call.'

'And who initiated that?'

'Daryl did. Well, I wanted to do it too, it's just I'd been putting it off for a while.'

'Why?'

Ellie seems a little shy about answering that question, but I ask her again until she does.

'I was just worried he might see me and then lose interest.'

'Why would he do that?'

'I don't know. He's some hot guy in California. Why would he be interested in me?'

'Because you're beautiful,' I say, but Ellie just screws her face up at that. 'Have you asked him why he likes you?' I enquire.

'Yeah, loads of times.'

'And what does he say?'

'He says because I make him laugh, and he likes talking to me.'

That sounds like a nice answer, but I'm not giving this guy a complete pass yet.
'So what do you two talk about?' I ask, curious as to how this long-distance thing has been working.
'At first, it was just life, you know, like what we do for work and stuff.'
'What does he do?'
'He works at a bike shop downtown,' Ellie replies, and her use of the word 'downtown' shows me how a little American slang is already creeping in.
'Okay, and then what?'
'We just got to know each other more. I guess the thing that really drew me to him was finding out he'd lost a parent too.'
'He has?'
'Yeah, his mum.'
'Did he tell you that after you told him about your dad?'
'No, he said it first.'
I think about that but guess it's okay. I was worried that he might have just been trying to exploit Ellie's grief by pretending to be just like her but if he mentioned that first, then that's less likely to be the case.
I have several more questions, all of which I ask but all of which Ellie has perfectly good answers for - questions about his family, his education and his interests. That's why, in the end, I realise I might have overreacted slightly when I first found out about Daryl.
'Okay, well, he sounds like a nice guy,' I admit, although I'm reserving full judgement because I still haven't met him properly and neither has my daughter.

'But there is the issue of him being all the way over there and you being all the way over here.'

'I know,' Ellie admits, looking downbeat. 'It's far.'

'Yes, it is.'

'But what if we could make it work?'

'What do you mean?'

'I mean, what if, even with the distance, we can find a way to be together. He makes me happy, Mum, he really does. This is the happiest I've been since Dad died.'

While that warms my heart to hear, it also makes me feel sad, not just because my daughter has been unhappy for so many years, but because she has been feeling like she has to keep her new-found happiness a secret from me.

'That's good, darling,' I say because, of course, it is. 'But I'm just trying to be practical here. You're in England, and he's in America. Realistically, I'm not sure how it could work.'

'One of us would probably have to move,' Ellie says suddenly, as if she's had a plan all along.

'What?'

'One of us would have to move to the other person's country so we could be together properly,' Ellie goes on as if what she is saying is so simple and doesn't involve one person completely uprooting their lives for the other.

'What? You two haven't even met each other yet, not properly, and you're talking about one of you moving?'

'We'd have to meet first, of course,' Ellie says, and then she looks like she has one more thing to add but hesitates before saying it.

'What is it?' I ask nervously.

'I was thinking, maybe, if it's okay, I could go over and see him in LA,' Ellie says before looking at me with hopeful eyes.

'You want to go to America to see this guy?'

'Yeah, why not?'

'Why not? Because it's dangerous! Because I don't know who he is! Because anything could happen to you over there!'

'Relax, he's not some psycho killer.'

'Isn't he? How do you know that for sure?'

'Because I've spoken to him and if you spoke to him too, then you'd see that he's a nice guy.'

'Okay, then prove it,' I say, putting that to the test.

'How?'

'I want to speak to him. Set up a video call. It's time I met this Daryl.'

Ellie looks surprised at my request, but I just fold my arms to show her that I'm not going to entertain any more talk of her going over there to meet this man unless I can see him for myself.

6

DAWN

I've had to wait until mid-afternoon before I've got somewhere with my wish to see Daryl on a video call, allowing for the time difference that exists between our two sections of the planet. But now the sun has risen on the west coast of America, Daryl is awake and after Ellie messaged him to tell him that I'd like to have a video chat with him, he has surprisingly agreed.

Now, all we need to do is get connected.

'I'm nervous,' Ellie admits as she logs in to whatever video call application she uses on her laptop.

'You're nervous now? Just wait until you're a parent,' I reply before picking up my cup of tea and taking an anxious gulp.

The truth is that while Ellie might be worried that I might be about to do something to embarrass her in front of her 'boyfriend', there is no way she can be anywhere near as worried as I am at present. She's my girl, my pride and joy and always will be, and pretty much the only thing I have left in this world. So with all that considered, how can I be anything but nervous about her and this new man she wishes to go and meet so many miles away?

I want her to be happy, but first, I want to know she is safe.

I guess we are about to find out.

The laptop bleeps and a second later, the screen displays live footage of a young man sitting in a bedroom.

I guess this is Daryl.

Judging him instantly on appearances, because that's what we all do before we get to know somebody, I note his tanned and handsome face, as well as the curls of blonde hair stuffed beneath a blue baseball cap, and immediately, I can see why my daughter likes this guy so much. There aren't many boys who look like him around here.

He looks athletic too, broad shoulders and toned arms, and at first, I suspect he might be a 'jock', that American term for the popular kid at school who played in all the sports teams and had the pick of all the girls. But then he smiles awkwardly when he sees us staring back at him, and I get the sense that while he might look like the coolest guy in town, he is a little shy and awkward and that makes him more endearing than if he was some cocky, confident Californian.

'Hey!' Ellie says, and I glance at my daughter sitting beside me and see the big smile that has spread across her face now that Daryl is on screen.

'Hi!' he says, and even though it was only one word, I detect the strong American twang in his voice.

'This is my mum,' Ellie says, and I guess that's my cue to speak.

Why do I feel so nervous?

'Hi, Daryl,' I say, doing my best to appear friendly and non-judgemental.

'Hello, Mrs Andrews,' Daryl replies, being ultra-polite by using my surname, but Ellie tells him that 'Dawn' will be just fine, which I guess it will.

'How's the weather over there?' Daryl asks next, which I guess is as good a conversation starter as any.

'Cold and wet, again,' Ellie moans before Daryl tilts his camera so we can see his bedroom window and when he does, we see nothing but sunlight streaming in.

'It's going to be another hot one here,' he says casually as if it's just another typical day in LA, which I guess it is.

'Whereabouts in Los Angeles are you?' I ask him, eager to learn as much as I can about this young man.

'Granada Hills. It's in the north of the city, in the San Fernando Valley.'

I have absolutely no idea where that is but nod my head as if I could pinpoint it on a map if I really had to.

'It looks amazing,' Ellie confirms. 'I've been looking at it online. Some of the houses are huge!'

'Yeah, there are some wealthy people around here,' Daryl confirms with a smile. 'But we've got a pretty modest home, really.'

'Modest? Are you kidding? You've got a swimming pool!' Ellie cries, and if I had any doubts as to how enamoured she was by the thought of the golden shores of Western America, then it has been removed now.

'A swimming pool? Wow,' I say, impressed but still sceptical because while Daryl might have a very different life to us, all I care about is his character. That's why I steer us onto a more sensible topic.

'Ellie tells me that you went to university,' I say, interested in learning more about his education.

'Yeah, that's right. Texas A & M. Home of The Aggies!' Daryl says before pointing to a maroon and white jersey that hangs from a shelf behind him. I guess they are a baseball team or something, but then Ellie informs me that they play American football.

'What was it you studied?' is my next question.

'Mechanical engineering.'

That sounds very impressive, but just like the location of his house or the identity of his favourite team, I have absolutely no idea what it actually means.

'Daryl likes working with cars and bikes,' Ellie informs me.

'Oh, like a mechanic?' I say, but Daryl doesn't look particularly impressed with that assumption.

'Not quite,' he tells me. 'I suppose it's similar. Just a little more complicated. I'm currently working in a motorcycle shop, and my job is to look at how they can make the vehicles they sell more efficient. But really, I want to go and work for one of the big manufacturers one day. Harley Davidson or someone like that.'

I've heard of them, so I nod my approval, and I guess Daryl seems to have his career path figured out, which is a promising start.

Ellie helps fill in some of the silences that occasionally follow then, asking Daryl to tell me all about life in California, ranging from where he grew up in the south of the city, closer to the coast, but moved further north when his dad got a new job. I hear all about his father, Harvey, and his role at a nearby research facility to his love of the Los Angeles Dodgers baseball team. But it's what I don't hear that is perhaps more telling. There is no mention yet of Daryl's mother, Jodie, although sadly, I know why that is. But just as I'm beginning to think that Daryl might not mention it as he gives me the rundown on his life, no doubt already prepped by Ellie earlier that this is what I would be seeking, he does go and mention her.

'Things changed a lot when we lost my mom,' Daryl admits, his warm smile fading and a sudden sadness emanating from him through the screen. 'I was away at university when she died, and it was a massive shock. Dad and I are doing okay now, but it never really gets easier, I guess.'

Daryl didn't have to tell me that because I have first-hand experience of such a thing too, but just hearing him talk like this makes it easy to see why this boy, out of the no doubt numerous ones who have messaged Ellie on that app, has risen to the top of the pile. Like my daughter at her best, he's fun and friendly but like her in her darkest moments, he is also broken and no doubt looking for something to fill that void in his heart.

As am I.

Then Daryl acknowledges another tricky subject; this one being the fact that he and Ellie are worlds apart.

'Look, I know it's not normal for two people to meet online and fall in love,' he says, the mention of the 'L' word causing Ellie to blush a little when he says it.

'But I just want you to know that whatever happens, I think your daughter is great, and I hope that one day we can meet each other and be together. I'm happy to come over there if that would be easier.'

'No way, I want to see LA first!' Ellie cries, and she turns to me to see what I think about that.

Before I have a chance to give my input, Daryl has something else to say that might help persuade me that letting my daughter go over to America doesn't have to be a huge problem.

'I've spoken to my dad about Ellie, and he's offered to pay for her flight here,' Daryl tells me, which sounds very generous of him. 'And once she is here, she's got free accommodation. She can stay here. We'll go to the beach, maybe to a Dodger's game.'

'I want to see all the celebrity mansions!' Ellie exclaims like an excited tourist who is already on her way.

But that's the thing. She isn't going there yet because I haven't said it's okay for her to. She might be twenty-four, but she lives in my house, and she is still my responsibility.

I lost Sean already.

I'm not risking losing my daughter too.

'What do you say, Mum?' Ellie asks me, her face lit up like Sunset Boulevard. 'Can I go and stay with Daryl in LA?'

I look from my daughter to the young man on the laptop screen and back again before I realise I have an answer for them both.

'Okay, you can go,' I say to Ellie, giving her what she wants. 'But I'm coming with you.'

7

ELLIE

I can't believe it. I'm going to LA to see Daryl! I'm so excited! California, here I come!

I put my pen down for a moment as another bout of adrenaline courses through me. I'm buzzing, but it's no different to how I've been feeling ever since the video call ended and Mum said she had no problem with me going. Even if she had, it wouldn't have made a difference. I'd have found a way to go anyway. There's no way I'm staying here all summer when I could be in America with the man I love. But it's much easier that Mum agrees that I can go because that means less arguing here.

But there is one catch.

Mum wants to come too.

I was shocked when she suggested that earlier, almost as shocked as Daryl. Both of us looked at each other through the screen and didn't really know what to say. But Mum was adamant she wanted to come, although she initially made out like it was only because she hadn't had a holiday in a long time and needed a break. But then, once we'd ended the call and Daryl was no longer able to listen in to our conversation, Mum told me the truth.

She wanted to come with me to make sure I was safe.

Of course, I told her that she was being silly because I'm not a kid anymore and there is nothing to worry about. As well as telling her that she wouldn't be demanding to come with me if I was going backpacking to Australia or Thailand like other people my age do, I reminded her that she'd already met Daryl, at least online anyway, and could see that he was a nice guy. She'd also heard about his dad, Harvey, too, and so knows there's nothing to worry about there either. Then there's the fact that they live in one of the safest parts of Los Angeles, where even a few celebrities choose to have their homes, so what's the big deal? I even said I might be safer there than I am here in this town, where teenagers roam the streets with knives and burglaries are a common problem.

But Mum wasn't buying it. She said she comes too or I don't go at all, so barring me sneaking out of the house to try and get to the airport to board a flight without her catching me, I don't have much choice. Then again, at least it means I won't have to be on my own all the way there. I'd probably get lost in the airport or maybe even get on the wrong plane by accident, but I won't have to worry about that with Mum next to me.

I'm going to Beverly Hills! Santa Monica! Sunset Boulevard! Arghhhh, I can't wait.

My latest diary entry is just a jumble of my excited thoughts as I contemplate my upcoming trip to The States, but I have a feeling the words in my diary are only going to get even sillier as the trip gets closer. We have booked our flights for next Tuesday because that was the cheapest day to fly and also because Mum couldn't get time off from work any sooner than that. As for my restaurant job, I've told Mum they have allowed me to have unpaid leave but in reality, they said if I go, then I won't have a role to come back to. I guess they thought they were putting me in a difficult position and assumed that I would ultimately choose to keep my waitressing job, but screw them. I told my boss that I quit, and it sure felt good to say those words, just like it feels good to know I won't ever have to set foot in that damn restaurant again. Okay, so I haven't told Mum about that part yet but she doesn't need to know. And maybe she never will because what if I decide to stay in America? If I don't come home, then it doesn't matter that I have no job back here anymore.

Could it happen? Could I stay in California with Daryl? I think that's the dream, although we'd probably have to get married for me to be able to get a visa and stay there.

A shot-gun wedding, perhaps.

How far is Las Vegas from LA?

Life feels so fun again. Is this what I've been missing all this time? Mum always wanted me to get out of bed and open my curtains and do something with my day, but she just didn't realise that there was nothing for me to do here. But there is so much opportunity in America. I could do anything, be anything, experience anything. I feel like I'm reborn, and I know when I step off that plane and see Daryl that I'll finally be happy again.

I just wish Dad were here. I bet he'd love LA. He'd get on well with Harvey. They would drink beer and talk about the difference between English and American sports. Dad would say it's football, not

soccer, while Harvey would probably try to get him into baseball. And he'd love the weather over there too. He always was a sun seeker.

I wish he was here for Mum too. The pair of them could go and have a date night in the city. I feel bad for Mum. She must be lonely. I was lonely too until I met Daryl. But at least she has this trip to look forward to. Maybe it's not such a bad thing she is going. It might bring us closer together. Maybe…

I am more than a little anxious about the fact that Mum is coming with me because I'd hate for this all to be ruined by the two of us arguing while we're there. I just want to focus on Daryl and making it work with him and won't have time for Mum and her drama. That's why I've made her promise not to cause any.

But we'll see about that.

I put my diary down and pick up my laptop before browsing a few online stores, looking at bikinis and swimsuits and short skirts and summery tops. It's going to be over thirty degrees in LA, way hotter than it ever gets here, so I need to be prepared for that. There's the pool and the beach and all those hot nights to think about.

Goodbye, raincoats and jeans.

Hello, dresses and sunglasses.

I feel like I want to buy a whole new wardrobe for this trip, and maybe I need to, but the problem is paying for it all. I've got some money saved up from my waitress job, but I don't want to blow through all of it before I've even got to America. I know Daryl has told me he will pay for everything when I get there, but I don't want him to think that I don't have my own money. I'm a fierce, independent woman, or at least I want him to think I am.

I guess I could ask Mum for some money to buy me these clothes, but she's already spending so much on flying to America herself. I told her she didn't have to come but she insisted, although that hasn't stopped her telling me several times how expensive it is to get out there. Mum was even crazy enough to get me to tell Daryl that his dad shouldn't have to pay for my flight and she would sort it out herself, only to see how much airfares were online and backtrack on that. Now Daryl, or at least Daryl's dad, is paying for my flight while Mum is covering her own. I'm super grateful for that, but it's still going to be an expensive trip either way, which explains why Mum is already back at work, taking another overtime shift to raise some last-minute cash.

I guess she needs a change of scene as much as I do. She hasn't stopped working since Dad died, and even though we always needed the money, I know it's also because it keeps her busy. Stops her from feeling sad. Prevents her from lying in bed all day with the curtains closed like I do.

Maybe Mum will be a new person after a little time in the sun.

She is right.

She does need a break.

I just hope she gives me and Daryl a break when we're over there.

8

DAWN

Airports always make me anxious. There's just too much going on in them. Time-conscious passengers rushing to get to their gate, dragging luggage behind them and bumping into other passengers who are running just as late for their flights. Pilots and cabin crew strolling through the chaos in their pristine uniforms and looking calm and serene yet also aware that they are the ones responsible for getting all these other people to their destinations safely. And then there's the myriad of things that every air traveller has to negotiate before they even get on their plane, from baggage check-in to boarding pass printouts to security shenanigans, and all that is before having to try and make sense of the giant electronic screens that show all the flights and which gate they are departing from.

Don't get me wrong, going abroad is great.

It's just getting out of the country that is the tricky part.

'Did you pack this suitcase yourself?' the burly middle-aged man on the other side of the counter asks me immediately after Ellie and I have just spent half an hour queuing up to approach him.

'Yes, of course,' I reply. 'My daughter was hardly going to do it for me.'

I laugh at my own joke but then realise it was ill-timed because airports are no places for jokes. That becomes even more obvious when the man behind the counter retains his grumpy expression before asking me where I'm flying to today.

'Los Angeles,' I confirm. 'The City of Angels, I believe they call it.'

That fun little fact has just as little an impact on the airport employee as my joke before it, and Ellie gives me a nudge to get my attention.

'Relax,' she tells me, clearly having realised how nervous I am, and I try to take her advice, opting to keep my mouth shut and only answer all future questions with as little fuss as possible.

But while I manage to avoid making any more bad jokes or offering useless bits of information to people who don't need them, it is hard to relax. I never used to be a nervous flyer, but it's been several years since I've been on a plane, so the butterflies are swirling in my stomach as we pick up our boarding passes and watch our suitcases gliding away on the conveyor belt to be put onto the plane. Then there's the fact that this is going to be such a long flight, over eleven hours in total, which will easily be the furthest I have ever travelled from home. And last but not least, there is the rather unique and unusual set of circumstances that surround the reason for this trip in the first place.

This isn't a typical holiday. It's something else; something I'm not even quite sure how to describe.

Is it just a short trip so my daughter can see someone she likes before we come back home and get on with the rest of our lives?

Or is it the beginning of what might be a very big change, resulting in life being very different for us all by the time all the travelling is over?

What if Ellie likes Daryl even more after this? What if she wants to stay or move out to America permanently? What if my daughter lives in California forever and this is the kind of trip I have to make every year just so I can see her?

It's all very unpredictable and nerve-racking and that's even before I seriously consider how unpredictable and nerve-racking it is to get inside a giant aluminium tube and be hurtled hundreds of miles an hour through the sky, thousands of feet above the ocean.

I know exactly what I'm going to do once I've got through security.

I'm going to buy a strong drink.

Thankfully, there are no dramas getting through the important checkpoint, and once it's clear I am not going to be arrested and accused of being an international terrorist plotting to bring death and destruction to the West, I can breathe a small sigh of relief. It's two hours until our flight now, which means we have a little time to browse in Duty Free and get some refreshments, not that I want to spend too much money before we board the plane.

That's because this trip is already expensive enough as it is.

It was lovely of Daryl, or at least Daryl's dad, to offer to pay for Ellie's flights because there is no way I could have paid for her and me to go together. I wouldn't want her to go alone and stay with some people whom I can't say I trust yet, but with them taking care of one side of the airfare, it just left my ticket to be paid for. There was no way I was going to expect Harvey to pay for that too, so I used what limited funds I have in my account to book my own flight. The problem is that leaves me little when I get back, at least until my next payday from the supermarket, although even then, it's hardly much.

I'm trying to stay positive and think about what all my friends said to me when I told them I was going to be accompanying Ellie on her love-fuelled quest to California. They told me that I deserved to do something fun and that I shouldn't let money worries completely rule my life. I, more than anyone, know how it's the memories that matter, not the money, and after the girls gave me a pep talk along those lines, I could see that I needed to do this not just to make sure Ellie is safe, but also for myself.

I'm still relatively young, and I'm in good health. I should appreciate that and make the most of it instead of spending every minute of my life toiling away at work and worrying about something in the house. I know Ellie is hoping this trip is going to change her life forever, but maybe it just might change mine too. I might come back with a new outlook on the world, feeling more positive or even just well-rested.

But we'll see about that.

I manage to make it past all the Duty-Free shops without Ellie getting me to open my purse and spend some of the travel money I have budgeted for this trip, and once we have sat down at a table in a fast-food restaurant and ordered an unhealthy but tasty meal, I am feeling a little calmer. Ellie is now the one who is amped-up, although she is excited rather than nervous, and she is constantly texting Daryl on her phone in between showing me photos of LA in her travel guide and stuffing chips into her mouth in between.

I'm glad that she is no longer in a mood with me over my decision to accompany her to America to meet Daryl and his family. While I expected some resistance when I first floated the idea, I had hoped she would back down and thankfully, she has. Of course, I did my best to get that to happen by telling her exactly what I was afraid of, which was her going to America alone, finding out Daryl was a complete weirdo or some actor working for somebody else and the next thing she knows, Ellie is locked up in some basement in a house in the desert, never to be seen again.

Okay, maybe I've read a few scare stories online and seen one too many horror movies in my youth, but I'd never forgive myself if I let my daughter willingly fly off to what turned out to be her doom so at least if I'm with her, I can make sure everything is okay.

Or the two of us end up locked up in a basement in the desert together.

One or the other.

These circumstances might be strange, but it is good to see Ellie so happy, and I have to remember how magical young love can be. Right now, Ellie's heart is beating not just for her, but for somebody else too, another person whom she feels connected to and who she probably thinks she couldn't live without. Just like how I was when I started dating Sean.

The romance. The lust. The possibility of it all.

I can't blame Ellie for falling in love with somebody.

I just wish it was somebody a little closer to home.

We manage to kill the last bit of time before our boarding call comes, and then, as I make my way onto the plane with the other two-hundred-or-so passengers departing these shores, I swallow hard and tell myself that everything is going to be okay.

The last time I went to America, Sean was strapping himself into the seat beside me while Ellie was on the other side of him, right by the window where she wanted to be so she could get the first glimpse of Florida.

Now it's just the two of us preparing to fly over the Atlantic.

But will it be the two of us coming back?

Or will I be coming home alone?

9

ELLIE

This flight is sooooooo long. We've been going for ten hours now, and we're still not there yet. I keep staring at the screen on the back of the seat in front of me, watching the 'Time To Destination' counter dwindling and willing the numbers to get smaller faster, but I guess I just have to be patient. I also have to remember that with every second that goes by, this plane is taking me another mile closer to Daryl.

A slight bump of turbulence distracts me from my diary, but as I look up around the cabin, I see it wasn't enough to worry anybody else or even wake them up. Most of the people I'm flying with are asleep, their eye masks pulled down over their faces and the window blinds shut beside them, making this cabin as dark as possible. We're flying through the day, not that it feels like it with how gloomy it is in the cabin, and it's only the little light above my head that is allowing me to see my diary in front of me.

But I turn the light off and decide I've made enough diary entries for one day. While it's helped me kill some time on this flight, I know there is nothing else for me to say in it until we get there.

I'm bored of writing about what it might be like to be with Daryl.

My next diary entry will be talking about what it's actually like to be with Daryl.

I put my diary away and fold my tray table back into its upright position before settling back in my seat and resuming the movie I've been watching on the in-flight entertainment. I picked it purposely because it's a rom-com set in LA, so I hope it is quite apt for what my life is going to be like soon, and as I put my headphones back on, I try to stay calm and not get too excited again.

A quick glance to my left tells me that Mum is still sleeping, her own eye mask on and her head resting back with a small pillow behind it, and I'm glad she is at peace. She's certainly a lot calmer than she was during the first few hours of the flight when she was jabbering away about all sorts of things, from whether or not our luggage had made it onto the plane correctly to what each bump of turbulence might have meant for the plane's capacity to get us there safely. But she soon calmed down once the cabin crew had brought the drinks trolley around, and after a couple of miniature bottles of red wine, she stopped stressing and learnt to enjoy this experience.

Flying can be boring and even a little scary, but it can also be fun. There are movies to watch, food and drink to enjoy, and it's one of the rare times when a person can get away from the craziness of the internet. There's no wi-fi on this plane and while that's annoying because it means I can't message Daryl or check my social media accounts, it's nice to not be on my phone every five minutes.

But saying that, ten hours is more than long enough to be uncontactable, so I do wish this plane would hurry up and land so I can get back online.

The next half an hour passes slowly as I watch the movie, but the action on screen is interrupted suddenly when the pilot comes over the intercom and announces that we will shortly be starting our descent into Los Angeles.

The lights in the cabin are turned on, and everyone who was sleeping before the announcement slowly starts to wake up, including Mum, who stirs in her seat beside me. She peels off her eye mask and looks around the cabin as if she's momentarily confused as to where she is, before she remembers that, yes, she is 38,000ft above North America.

'How long was I asleep for?' Mum asks me as she rubs her neck and tries to stretch as much as the tight seating space in here will allow.

'About three hours,' I reply, slightly envious that Mum and so many other people on here have been able to sleep for a big portion of this flight while I've been wide awake for all of it.

'We're almost there,' Mum says in her sleepy state, and I confirm that we are.

As I see the cabin crew going around making sure all the tray tables are up and the window blinds are open again, I realise this is getting very real now. We're almost in LA and that means it's almost time for me to meet Daryl properly.

No more messaging. No more video calls. No more distance between us.

Nothing getting in the way of us actually touching each other.

I almost wish there was a little more time left on this flight because now I'm seriously tempted to get one of those miniature bottles of red wine from the trolley to calm my own nerves. But the cabin crew aren't serving refreshments anymore, they are preparing the plane for landing, just like the pilots in the cockpit who will be running through their landing routines at this very moment.

I have no idea how anybody can be clever enough to fly a plane from one country to another, and I'm glad it doesn't have to be a concern of mine. I've got enough on my plate with going to meet Daryl and pretty soon, I'll be with him. He's meeting us at the airport, as is his dad, and the plan is for them to drive us back to their house. Then I guess it's all about talking and getting to know each other more, which might be a bit uncomfortable, especially with Mum with me, but it is what it is.

I hope Mum gets along with Harvey but more importantly, I hope she gets along with Daryl. I need her to like him because I like him. Otherwise, this trip could get very awkward, very fast.

My ears pop as the plane lowers its altitude, and Mum offers me some sweets to chew on, a sure-fire way to help alleviate some of the pressure in my ears. I also yawn a couple of times to help with that too, and as the cabin keeps dropping, I know we're almost there now.

That becomes even more apparent when I look out of the window and catch a glimpse of the sprawling city below me. Los Angeles stretches out for miles in every direction, and as I stare at all the tiny buildings below, I see swimming pools and tennis courts, not to mention numerous cars queuing on busy highways. I also see the mountains that surround this city, solid structures of rock that are nothing like we have back in England. Everything is either green or grey back home, but here, everything looks like it's bathed in a yellowish hue, the strong sun overhead scorching everything below it. Then I see a flash of blue, and in the distance, I realise I can see the sea. I'm not close enough to make out the beach, but I know there are numerous stretches of sand down there somewhere too.

Venice Beach. Santa Monica. Malibu. All the places I've gawked at when I've seen them in my favourite American reality shows.

It all looked like paradise.

And now I'm here in paradise myself.

An electronic whirring sound fills the cabin then but it's just the noise of the wheels lowering beneath the plane, and as the ground comes sharply up to meet us, the whole cabin bumps as we make impact with the ground. But it's a perfect landing, and as the plane begins to slow quickly, I get my first glimpse of LAX, the famous airport that welcomes visitors to this sun-kissed city.

'I can't believe we're actually here,' I say to Mum, and for a second, I feel like I might have to reach for the brown paper bag that is tucked into the back of the seat in front of me. It's a bag that is there in case a passenger feels nauseous during the flight, but it's not the flying that is making me queasy.

It's the knowledge that Daryl is inside that airport now, waiting to see me emerge through the Arrival gate.

'Everything's going to be okay,' Mum suddenly says to me, taking my hand, and I guess she can see how anxious I am now that we've landed. 'Whatever happens, I'm here.'

In that moment, I'm glad Mum volunteered herself to accompany me to America because even though it felt uncool and somewhat unnecessary to have her by my side, it now feels quite nice.

Mum's right. Everything is going to be okay. Then again, Mum has said that before. She said it when Dad was sick, and things weren't okay in the end there.

So what if Mum's wrong again?

What if everything isn't going to be okay here?

What if coming here was a big mistake?

It's too late to go back now.

The plane has stopped.

The doors are opening.

And now I'm minutes away from meeting Daryl.

10

DAWN

Crossing numerous time zones always leads to a little confusion on the part of a traveller and I'm getting another example of that here as I set my watch to Los Angeles time. But it's weird because despite boarding the plane in England on Tuesday afternoon and flying for half a day, it's still Tuesday afternoon when I get off it here.

'It's definitely eight hours behind, right?' I ask Ellie again as I sleepily shuffle alongside her towards the customs checkpoint.

'Yep,' Ellie says, clearly impatient for this line to move quicker than it is. 'It's three-thirty.'

'It'll soon be midnight back home,' I note but acknowledging such a thing is hardly going to help me deal with any jet lag that might occur soon.

The queue is slow, but we get to the front eventually and when we do, we're met by a serious-looking woman in a uniform that looks both impressive and scary, which is probably the intention.

'Passports,' the gruff female U.S. border patrol official says, and Ellie and I can't comply with that command quickly enough, handing over our respective travel documents and hoping that everything is in order so that we aren't turned around and put back on the first flight home, not that we should be, but you never know, do you?

'What's the purpose of your visit?' the official asks us.

'Leisure,' I say because it's either that or business, and this is definitely not a business trip. But Ellie decides to nervously expand on that point.

'I'm going to meet my boyfriend for the first time,' she says with a beaming smile to match. But there is no smile forthcoming from the customs official. Instead, all there is are several questions that we could probably have avoided if Ellie had just stayed quiet.

'What is your boyfriend's name?'

'Is he an American citizen?'

'How did you get in contact with him?'

'What is his address?'

'Will you be staying there for the duration of your visit?'

Ellie is required to answer each question quickly and while I try to help her because she seems to be getting more nervous the longer this conversation goes on, the official only ever looks at my daughter and not me.

There's a very brief but frightening moment when I fear we might have to face more questions elsewhere, possibly in a small, private room where two men smoking cigarettes will point a bright lamp in our faces and demand to know if we are international spies coming here to steal state secrets. But thankfully, that's just my imagination running away with itself and a second later, the inquisitive official stamps our passports, forces a smile onto her face and tells us to enjoy our stay.

I'm not sure if there was really any need for the 'tough cop' routine but it's over with now, and as Ellie and I scurry towards the baggage carousel, we are relieved to be on the other side of the checkpoint. I guess we're officially in America now, with no more questions to face, but before we can actually get out of this busy airport, we need to find our suitcases.

More nerves follow as we wait for what feels like an age for our luggage to slowly come around on the carousel, but after spending twenty minutes imagining our suitcases sitting in the airport in London because somebody didn't do their job properly, we find them and haul them away.

But even after all that stress, the most stressful part is still to come.

We now have to find Daryl and Harvey at the Arrivals section of LAX, one of the busiest airports in the world.

'I feel like I'm going to be sick,' Ellie admits as we head towards the sliding doors through which all arriving passengers have to go through on their way out.

'It'll be okay,' I say to reassure her but deep down, I can't say for certain that it will be. Sure, we'll probably find the two men we are looking for, but there's no guarantee things will go well when we do.

As the doors slide open and we step out, I'm prepared to come face to face with Daryl and his dad. But in reality, I come face to face with hundreds of people, all of whom are eagerly waiting for their loved ones to arrive, and suddenly, finding the people we are here to see feels akin to finding a needle in a haystack.

'How are we going to spot them?' I ask as I scan the faces of numerous people, from grandparents to husbands and wives, children, taxi drivers, shuttle bus drivers and on and on.

'He said he'd hold up a sign for us,' Ellie replies, so we start scanning the crowd for anything with our name on it. But it feels like a futile task, or at least it does until Ellie suddenly grabs my arm and lets out an excited shriek.

'He's over there!'

Looking at where my daughter is pointing, it takes me a moment before I see the large cardboard sign with our names on it being held up by two men.

Ellie & Dawn Andrews - Welcome to America!

Accompanying the words are all sorts of colourful drawings, from the red, white and blue star-spangled banner of the American flag to a circular, orange shape, which I presume is the sun, and a blue, squiggly line, which I guess signifies the sea. The sign is a very practical way of drawing our attention, but it's a cute gesture to include drawings alongside our names, as well as a very empathetic welcome, and as we approach the two men holding the sign, I feel like things have gotten off to a good start.

But we haven't spoken yet.

'Ellie!' Daryl cries as we get nearer, and he lets go of his half of the sign and rushes towards my daughter, his arms open wide in preparation for a hug.

Ellie is just as happy to see him and drops her suitcase before meeting him in the middle, and as the pair of them hug, I smile for a moment because it's obvious, if it wasn't already, that these two are crazy about each other.

'Young love, hey,' a male voice says, and I see Daryl's father, Harvey, walking towards me with his hand out. 'You must be Dawn. It's a pleasure to meet you.'

I would hate not to make a good first impression with this man, so I quickly take his hand and shake it. When I do, I notice his firm grip as well as his strong eye contact, and that's the first time I notice his dazzling blue eyes. Along with his crop of blonde hair, tanned skin and wide shoulders, I would say this man was very attractive, and I might even be tempted to flirt.

Or at least I would if there wasn't a chance I might end up related to him one day.

'Hi, Harvey. Lovely to meet you,' I say, smiling as widely as I can.

'How was the flight?'

'Not bad, actually.'

'Really? I flew to London once years ago, and it almost killed me.'

'Oh, right. Yeah, if I'm honest, I'm absolutely exhausted.'

'I bet you are. Don't worry, we'll get you back to our place, and you can have a good rest there.'

Harvey, like a true gentleman, offers to take my suitcase then and even though I initially resist, he persuades me to hand it over, lightening me of my burden.

'Thank you,' I say, but he tells me not to mention it, before the two of us turn our attention to the happy couple who are still hugging in front of us.

Harvey clears his throat then, a tactic to politely get their attention, and that's when Ellie and Daryl break off from their hug and remember the introductions aren't quite complete yet.

'Mrs Andrews. It's so nice to meet you!' Daryl exclaims before he comes towards me for a hug.

'You too!' I say before his strong arms envelop me.

I see Ellie and Harvey hug then as well before Harvey gestures to his son for him to relieve Ellie of her luggage too.

He does just that and then, with both our suitcases in the careful hands of the two men we have flown all this way to meet, Ellie and I follow them out of the airport, passing amongst the busy throngs of people all the way to the car park where Harvey's vehicle is located.

As we get there and I savour my first few moments being out in the California air, I have three initial observations about this place.

One, it's very hot.

Two, there are no clouds in the sky.

And three, I'm glad Harvey is going to be the one who drives us around here because the traffic looks absolutely crazy.

11

DAWN

What's the last thing a person needs after getting off an eleven-hour flight?

Getting stuck in a traffic jam outside the airport.

Fortunately, Harvey has somehow managed to negotiate the bumper-to-bumper pile of cars on the freeway and while it took a while, we are now leaving the congested inner city behind and heading into more open space.

As we navigated our way through this concrete jungle, Harvey and I made small talk in the front of the car while Ellie and Daryl sat together in the back, whispering sweet nothings to each other and holding hands the whole time. The parents in the front have mostly left the love sick youngsters in the back to it, but there have been a couple of occasions when Harvey and I have shared a knowing glance and rolled our eyes at all the displays of affection going on behind us.

As we exit yet another freeway and turn onto a wider but more traffic-free road, I notice that the houses are starting to get much bigger now on the other side of my window, and as we move on, the palm trees seem to be getting bigger too.

'We're almost there,' Harvey tells me when he notices me trying to stifle a yawn, but despite that sleepy behaviour, I actually feel quite awake. That's because I'm in awe of the neighbourhood we are now moving through.

'Oh my, these houses are huge,' I say as I stare out at them all passing us by, wondering how on earth anybody could ever earn enough money to afford one of these properties. This is a world away from the neighbourhood I grew up in or the neighbourhood I live in now.

'Yeah, they're not cheap, but they're worth every penny,' Harvey says as he holds a steady hand on the wheel and keeps us cruising. 'Crime is a big problem in certain parts of LA but not here, and paying for that peace of mind is important.'

I almost miss what he just said as I gawk at a huge white mansion set behind tall black gates with two sports cars on the driveway, but it doesn't matter because Harvey carries on anyway.

'Believe it or not, this isn't even one of the best neighbourhoods in the area,' he tells me as he turns a corner onto yet another street full of houses that are surely far too big for one family to ever need. 'I'll have to take you to Brentwood. That's where a lot of the rich and famous live. It makes this place look like downtown on a bad night.'

'I find that hard to believe,' I say as I look from one impressive home to the next. 'How long have you lived around here?'

'Ever since Daryl was small. We moved here when he was five. Much safer for him and far better schools than where we lived before. It's a lot nicer than where I grew up, and I wanted to give him a better start in life.'

That desire for a parent to want to give their child a better upbringing than the one they had is something I can relate to, although I've clearly had a much harder time doing that for Ellie than Harvey has had for Daryl. It's one thing to want to give your son or daughter the best of everything but it's quite another to actually be able to afford it, and despite my best efforts, I've never quite been able to say that I gave Ellie the best house in the best neighbourhood with the best schools. But she's turned out okay, I suppose, so I shouldn't be too hard on myself for that.

She's got manners and knows the difference between right and wrong and aren't they the most important things? Then again, looking around here, maybe swimming pools, sports cars, and houses with a dozen bedrooms are the only things that matter.

But then, all of a sudden, I get a glimpse that life in this part of the world might not be as perfect as it seems. That comes in the form of the missing person poster I spot taped to the side of a lamppost as we near it.

I notice the alarming headline ***HAVE YOU SEEN THIS WOMAN?*** above an image of a female who looks to be of a similar age to Ellie. Beneath that is the unsettling heading ***DESPERATE MOTHER SEEKING ANSWERS – PLEASE HELP ME FIND MY DAUGHTER*** and below that, I see the name ***AUBREE***. But then we pass the lamppost, and the poster disappears from view, although it's not out of my mind yet.

'Have they found that woman yet?' I ask Harvey as I notice another poster just like it taped to another lamppost up ahead.

'Unfortunately not,' Harvey replies as he maintains a steady pace. 'Such a shame.'

'How long has she been missing?'

'I'm not sure now. It's been a while.'

'Three months,' Daryl says from the back, and I guess he's not totally distracted with Ellie to listen to what we are talking about in the front.

'Did she live around here?' I ask, thinking about how Harvey just mentioned this was supposedly one part of the city where crime was not a problem.

'No, a different part of the city,' Harvey tells me.

'What do you think happened to her?' I ask as we pass the second poster, the startling sign taped up right outside a house that must be worth at least $5 million, making quite the juxtaposition.

'Nobody knows,' Harvey says with a sigh. 'I can't imagine what her poor mother is going through. She's been on television a couple of times. Making an appeal, that kind of thing. But so far, nothing.'

'Why are the posters here? Did she go missing in this neighbourhood?'

'Oh no, the posters are up all over the city,' Harvey says, but there's something about the speed with which he answered that which makes me wonder if it's true.

I feel unsettled as I ponder asking a few more questions about the poor woman who has seemingly vanished around here somewhere, but before I can say anything more, Daryl tells Ellie that we are here.

'Welcome to our place,' he says, and as the car slows down, I look ahead at the property right in front of us through the windscreen.

It's not quite as big as some of the homes we have passed to get here but that doesn't mean it's not impressive in its own right. A whitewashed property with a charming stone wall encircling it, I notice the small water fountain in the centre of the driveway as we pass through the gates and come to a stop. It's two storeys tall with a balcony outside one of the upper windows, and I wonder if that is the master bedroom. If so, the balcony is a nice feature because it would allow the owner of the house the option to get some fresh air shortly after waking up.

The lawn to my left is lush and green despite the searing temperatures here, though I guess it owes its thanks to the sprinkler system that is currently dousing it in water. To the left of the impressive front door is a double garage, and as we get out of the car, Harvey proudly tells me that he keeps two motorbikes in there, "his pride and joys" as he calls them, and clearly where his son got his love of two-wheeled vehicles from too.

The trickle of the water fountain on the driveway, combined with the sound from the sprinkler, is all very peaceful, although that peace is broken momentarily when Harvey and Daryl start wheeling our suitcases across the concrete.

Ellie discreetly mouths the word 'wow' to me as we follow the two men to the front door and I feel compelled to agree with her. But I'll reserve my judgement until I see the inside of this property.

It looks amazing on the outside, but appearances can be deceiving, can't they?

Never judge a book by its cover and all that.

Then the front door opens, and I get my first glimpse of the inside of the house.

That's when it's my turn to say wow to my daughter.

12

DAWN

'You have to show me the pool!' Ellie cries as soon as we step foot inside the spacious home.

'Of course! Right this way,' Daryl says, leading her through the large open-plan living area towards the set of glass double doors at the back.

As he slides them open and the pair step outside, I hang back with Harvey, who makes sure our suitcases are settled by the foot of the stairs before he turns to me and smiles.

'I'll give you the guided tour,' he says before gesturing to the sofas and flatscreen TV that hangs on the wall above them. 'This is the lounge. Make yourself at home here. Eat chips, watch a movie, relax.'

'Thank you,' I say before he opens a door and shows me into the kitchen.

'Wow, this is lovely,' I say as I marvel at the granite countertops, the large coffee machine and the impossibly big fridge that sits in the back corner beside a window that overlooks the garden.

'Are you a coffee drinker?' Harvey asks me when he sees my eyes lingering on the expensive-looking machine that has all manner of buttons and switches on it.

'I am,' I confirm, which makes Harvey's smile even wider before he tells me that I'm going to love the coffee that this machine can produce.

I glance through the window then and see Ellie and Daryl standing beside a very impressive pool. Then again, coming from where I do, every pool is impressive.

'Here,' Harvey says when he notices me looking outside, and he unlocks a back door before leading me out onto a sun-drenched patio where I notice two cushioned loungers stationed beside the pool.

'Oh my, this is wonderful,' I say, scarcely able to believe that this is somebody's back garden.

If I ever want to sunbathe beside a pool, then I have to fly to another country and pay hundreds of pounds to stay at a hotel, yet Harvey merely has to open his back door and he's got it all here.

'Can we go in?' Ellie asks as she kneels down and puts her hand in the water.

'Hell yeah, let's go get changed,' Daryl says, and he helps Ellie back up before they head for the house.

'Are you coming in, Mum?' Ellie asks me as she passes Harvey and me at the door.

'Oh, erm, I don't think I packed a swimsuit,' I say, feeling a little self-conscious about getting half-naked at a stranger's house, even though I know I definitely did pack suitable swimwear.

'That's okay. You could wear one of Mum's old ones,' Daryl says but when he does, I notice Harvey look uncomfortable at such a suggestion.

'Oh no, it's fine. Don't worry,' I say. 'I'm not much of a swimmer anyway. I'll be happy on one of the loungers.'

'No, don't be silly. It's fine,' Harvey says, though the expression on his face is still a little unconvincing. 'But first, let me show you to your bedrooms.'

We all go back inside, swapping the stifling heat of the outdoors for the cool air-conditioned interior of the lavish home, and as we climb the staircase, I wonder just how big my bedroom might be.

I get the answer to that question when Harvey shows me into the room that will be mine for the duration of my stay, and as Harvey drops my suitcase onto a double bed, he once again tells me to make myself at home before letting me know where the bathroom is. It's at the end of the hallway and is as decadent as I would have imagined, all gold taps, marble flooring and a bath that is almost as big as the pool outside. But the thing I'm most thrilled about is the fact that my bedroom seems to be the one that has access to that balcony I saw when we arrived earlier.

Unlocking the door that leads onto it, I step out and look down at the driveway below. But from this vantage point, I've also got a great view out over the rest of the neighbourhood and the hills beyond them.

This place really is something.

Curious to see what Ellie's bedroom is like, I go in search of her and find her in the room across the hallway from mine, although quite how long she plans on staying in there is another matter entirely. While I haven't discussed it with her yet, it's pretty obvious to me that she will be hoping to spend some time in Daryl's bed during this trip, and even though I know they are both grown adults, I'm not sure how I feel about that because this is still a very unusual situation and taking things slowly might be better. But rather than broach that tricky subject now, I just tell her that this place is lovely, though Ellie barely acknowledges me as she quickly unpacks her suitcase, pulling out a bikini that is much smaller than I would have liked her to wear.

'You're wearing that?' I ask her, even though it's obvious that is her plan because she is now starting to strip off, trading her baggy, warm English clothes for an outfit more befitting of the Californian climate.

'What's the problem?' she asks casually.

'I don't know. It's a little skimpy, isn't it?'

'So?'

'So, we're guests in someone else's house. Maybe cover up a little more.'

'I'm going swimming. I'm hardly going to wear lots of clothes for that, am I?'

'Last one in the pool is a loser!' Daryl calls from out in the hallway before I hear him heading downstairs, and that only makes Ellie speed up.

I'm still not thrilled about what she's wearing, not just because Daryl will see her like this but Harvey too and we still barely know either of them, but I decide to bite my tongue and say no more because I don't want the homeowner to hear his guests arguing already.

'See you down there,' Ellie says to me as she leaves the bedroom, and when she goes downstairs, I return to my own room and do a little unpacking of my own. But while it was polite of Harvey to tell me to make myself at home here, it's never as simple as that when a person is staying in someone else's house, is it? Despite Harvey's best intentions, making me feel welcome and giving me a great bedroom to sleep in, I still feel awkward as I take my items of clothing out of my suitcase and look for somewhere to store them to prevent them getting any more creased than they already are.

I open a few drawers and hang a few dresses on the hooks in the wardrobe, but my movements are tentative, the movements of someone who feels a bit like they are walking on those metaphorical eggshells. The truth is I can never be as comfortable here as I am in my own house, so it's pointless for me to even try to be. Sure, I might be able to unpack and even sit on a sun lounger with a cold drink as I watch my daughter splashing around in the pool, but I will still be far from at ease here and maybe I never will be.

It's a shame because from what I've seen so far, both Harvey and his son are lovely people, very polite and friendly, making the effort to chat with us both and put us at ease in these unfamiliar surroundings. But even with all that considered, this is still a highly unusual situation. Normally, when a parent meets their child's boyfriend or girlfriend for the first time, it will be for a short period, maybe an hour or two, over a meal or a simple drink. After that, depending on how the relationship goes, it could be a while before the parents actually meet each other. Even then, it would just be in a simple setting, possibly on neutral ground, at a restaurant perhaps, and for a short time once more. Over time, all the parties would get to know each other better and grow closer but it would be a slow and steady process, likely over many years, before one day, the children might decide to get married and the two families would come together to celebrate, no awkwardness between any of them at that point because they'd been gradually drip-fed into each other's lives over a long period.

But this is a unique situation, and now, after just meeting for the first time, I am going to be living with my daughter's boyfriend and his father 24/7 for the next week. I don't know anybody else who has had to do such a thing. Certainly, none of my friends had to do this when they met their children's partners and families. But here I am, miles from home, in this house, trying to somehow figure this out while I'm right in the middle of it.

That's very intense.

But as I continue to unpack my clothes and try and figure out what to wear for when I go down to the pool, I had no idea just how intense things were actually about to get.

13

DAWN

It takes me a few minutes of deep breaths and positive thinking before I leave the bedroom and rejoin the rest of the group and when I do, I find everybody by the pool, as I suspected. Ellie and Daryl are already in the water, both currently bobbing around with their heads and shoulders being the only parts of their bodies that aren't submerged. But Harvey isn't in the pool and I'm quite glad about that because it might mean I don't have to go in yet if I don't want to.

The man of the house is sitting in a white wicker chair beside a table, upon which sits two bottles. One is sunscreen, which seems sensible, while the other is Rosé, which may be less sensible because it's still the afternoon. That's why, after accepting Harvey's invitation to take a seat in the spare chair at the table, I make a point of reaching for the bottle with the SPF 30 logo printed on it rather than the bigger bottle with the fruity pink contents in it. But that doesn't stop Harvey from offering me something from the bottle I haven't touched yet.

'Care for a drink?' he asks me. 'The only problem is you'll have to drink out of a plastic cup. I made the mistake of bringing glass out here once, but I won't be doing that again in a hurry.'

Harvey picks up one of the plastic cups with the intention of pouring me a drink, but I politely decline.

'Maybe later,' I say before doing my best to stifle a yawn, though it's not one that Harvey fails to spot.

'Of course, you must be so tired,' he says sympathetically. 'Don't worry. Your body clock will sort itself out again soon enough.'

He reclines in his chair then and turns to watch our children in the pool and as I do the same, I notice both Ellie and Daryl already have their own cups of Rosé. It's not a problem because they're both old enough to drink. But considering they are two lustful youngsters together for the very first time, is adding alcohol to the equation really a wise idea? As if reading my mind, Harvey leans towards me across the table and lowers his voice.

'I hope you don't mind me pouring Ellie a drink,' he says. 'It's just she seems very nervous, as does Daryl, to be fair. I thought it might help take the edge off things for both of them so they can relax and enjoy being together a little more.'

'Oh, it's okay,' I reply, although I am wondering why Harvey thinks alcohol is the best way to lower inhibitions.

Isn't talking and getting to know each other while sober the healthiest way to do that for all of us?

'I admit to being a little nervous myself,' Harvey goes on, sitting back again but keeping his voice low so those in the pool won't be able to catch every word of our conversation.

'You're nervous?'

'Yeah. I mean, I obviously want Daryl and Ellie to get on well because I know how much this means to them. But I want us to get on well too.'

'You do?'

'Don't you?'

'Yes, of course!'

Maybe I should have accepted that offer of a drink because while everyone else here is easing their nerves with a little liquid refreshment, mine are still jangling. But Harvey offers me a warm smile, no doubt intended to put me more at ease before he attempts to find further common ground between us from which we can get to know each other better.

'So, tell me, and I want your honest answer on this one,' he says with a cheeky wink. 'How did you feel when you found out your daughter was in love with an American guy?'

I think about my answer for a second, not wanting to be too honest in case it comes across as offensive. If I was to tell the truth, then I'd have to say to Harvey that I was very concerned, initially assuming it was a joke when Ellie first told me, before going on to think that it was a stupid notion and that it possibly couldn't last. But somehow, I'm not sure he'd appreciate me saying those things, so I guess I'll be polite.

'Well, it was a bit of a shock, of course,' I say with an awkward chuckle. 'But I guess when it comes to matters of the heart, then anything can happen.'

'Okay, so that's the diplomatic answer,' Harvey says with a sly grin. 'Now, how about the truthful one?'

I hesitate because I'm not sure if Harvey is being serious or not. Thankfully, he breaks the tension quickly with a laugh.

'It's okay, you don't have to pretend to me. If you freaked out a little bit and thought the whole concept of an American guy and an English girl getting together online was crazy, then you're not alone. I was not happy at all when I first heard about it.'

Harvey's honesty helps put me at ease and to reward that, I eventually offer some honesty of my own.

'I was shocked,' I admit. 'And then I was worried. I want my daughter to be happy, but I just didn't see how a long-distance relationship like this one could ever work.'

'Me too. I asked Daryl why he couldn't just meet a girl from around here. Why did he have to go looking for love so far away?'

'Exactly!'

'But then I realised that it was just my fears and insecurities surfacing. I mean, why was I really bothered that my son had fallen in love? I should have been happy, right? Any father should be. But I was scared, and I guess it was because I was scared that I was going to lose him to another country.'

Harvey is continuing to be very honest with me, but it feels good to hear about his worries, too, because they are exactly like mine.

'I was the same,' I admit. 'I didn't want Ellie to move away and leave me behind.'

'It sucks to be scared as an adult, doesn't it?' Harvey says, and we share a laugh.

'It sure does.'

We watch the pair of happy youngsters swimming up and down in front of us for a moment before Harvey leans in and speaks again.

'But the main thing is that they are happy. Lord knows Daryl deserves some happiness after what he's been through. And I hope you don't mind me saying but I believe Ellie has suffered just as much as my son has when it comes to that.'

Harvey's gentle broaching of a sensitive subject is done carefully and I appreciate that.

'She's certainly suffered,' I say as I watch Ellie go under the water before bursting back up again and splashing Daryl as he floats beside her.

There's a moment then when I consider asking Harvey about his late partner but I quickly decide not to, not having the confidence to go into such a deep and awkward subject this early on. Harvey seems to be feeling the same way, too, because he doesn't say anything then either, though I notice his eyes are fixed on my hands and when I look down, I realise why.

It's because I'm anxiously twirling my wedding ring around on my finger.

I stop doing that as soon as I realise I've been doing it, and to quickly get our minds off such a heavy subject, I gesture towards the bottle of Rosé.

'I think I will have that drink, actually,' I say with a smile. 'It's night-time in the UK, after all.'

Harvey's face lights up then before he quickly pours me my drink, and as I accept the plastic cup, I still feel nervous but am starting to realise that I don't need to be. Harvey is lovely. He's a gentleman. But most of all, he's suffered like I have, and at the end of the day, he's just trying to do the right thing by his child. Regardless of what ends up happening between the two lovebirds in the pool, I will try to make whatever time we have together comfortable and enjoyable. But then Harvey speaks again and what he says makes my awkwardness quickly return.

'I guess it won't be long now until they sleep with each other.'

'Excuse me?' I ask, the first refreshing sip of Rosé almost catching in my throat.

'Oh, come on. I'm sorry to have to be blunt and point it out, but I think it's pretty obvious that Daryl and Ellie are going to want to get closer to each other during the course of your stay here.'

Harvey's eyes are on the pair in the pool and when I look at them, I see exactly what he is referring to because Daryl has his arms around Ellie, and they briefly look into each other's eyes for a lust-laden moment before he dunks her under the water to tease her.

'The way I see it, we either make a big deal out of it or we accept it,' Harvey goes on, his voice low again, although he probably wouldn't be heard by those in the pool anyway because Daryl is laughing loudly. 'They're both adults, so I say we treat them as such and let them stay in the same bedroom. They've been talking online for a while now, and now they're together in the same place, it's the next natural step for them.'

I guess Harvey is right, and I can't really disagree, though I would have liked to think that Ellie would take her time with Daryl and gradually get closer to him over the course of our trip here rather than just jump into bed with him on the first night.

'But that's just my opinion,' Harvey quickly says, holding up his hands. 'If you think they should be in separate bedrooms then that's fine. It's my house but she's your daughter, and I won't argue with you there. However, I can't promise the same for my son. He might be quite annoyed, as may Ellie.'

Harvey chuckles then before pouring himself another drink, and the two of us sit in silence for a little while, happy to let the kids in the pool entertain us for the time being. But they're far too busy entertaining themselves to notice their parents' eyes on them.

Ellie is happy; that is very clear to see.

That means I should be too.

So why can I still not shake that feeling in the pit of my stomach?

The one that tells me that I can't relax yet.

Just in case.

14

DAWN

We stayed out by the pool long enough for me to drink a little too much Rosé and enjoy a little too much sunshine. That's why I then spent half an hour in my room chugging from a bottle of water while applying moisturiser to my slightly pink face. But I'm back downstairs again now because it's time for mine and Ellie's first meal in this house, and judging by the food laid out on the table, Harvey and Daryl have gone to quite an effort to give us a dinner that will satisfy our sizeable appetites.

I see chicken wings and fries and pizza and bottles of cola, not to mention barbeque sauce, ketchup and a few other condiments with labels I don't recognise because they are American brands. Judging by the calorific treats on offer, it's obvious that Harvey is eager for us to enjoy our first meal Stateside, but I do hope it's just for the benefit of his British guests and that he and his son don't eat like this too often because it's hardly the healthiest assortment of things. But then, as we take our seats, Daryl offers me a little insight as to why his father has chosen to give us more of a fast-food meal than a proper home-cooked one.

'Dad's never been much of a chef,' he says as he pours himself a glass of cola before offering the bottle to Ellie.

'Hey, I'm not that bad, am I?' Harvey cries as he emerges from the kitchen and approaches the dining table with a plate that is piled high with onion rings.

'No, this is great,' I say because I'm so hungry I could eat anything, though I've always been impartial to a few unhealthy foods in my time anyway.

'Yeah, it's great, thank you,' Ellie says from her seat right beside Daryl, whose side she has not left since we got here.

Harvey seems to have decided that is enough food for the time being because he takes his seat next to me on my side of the table and then we all tuck in.

'Jodie used to do all of the cooking,' Harvey explains as I put a couple of chicken wings onto my plate. 'She had a real talent for putting a meal together. I never found cooking that interesting myself. To me, food is just fuel and the quicker I can get it in my belly and get on with the rest of my day, the better. But Jodie would spend hours in the kitchen preparing a meal. We used to host dinner parties for friends and neighbours. It was fun.'

I note the hint of sadness in Harvey's voice as he finishes his last sentence but decide not to dwell on it, instead opting to compliment him on what he has been able to put together for us tonight, even if his skills tend to lie elsewhere.

The conversation is somewhat basic then as we all tuck into our meals, just a few mentions of things of interest in the area before Ellie and I field some questions about what there is to do in the area where we live back home. But the consensus from my daughter is that there is very little to do around where we are from while there are much more exciting options available to the people who live here, and to be honest, I have to agree, though I do my best to make my little slice of English life sound a little more interesting than it is.

'I guess there are pros and cons to every place,' Harvey muses as he puts a couple more fries onto his fork. 'We get better weather over here, and it sure is nice to be able to go to the beach whenever we want to. But on the other hand, we have a big problem with homelessness. And then there's the issue of guns. It seems we're never far away from another mass shooting being in the news.'

I admit that firearms and the ease at which they can be misused in this country must be a concern for many Americans, and I ask a few questions then about how Harvey, and indeed Daryl, handle living with such a threat lurking in the background.

'You just get used to it,' Daryl says with a shrug. 'Lots of people have guns here but most people use them correctly.'

'Yeah, I bet people having guns must seem crazy to you Brits but over here, citizens carrying firearms is as normal as rainy weather and green fields are to you guys,' Harvey adds with a chuckle.

'Do you have a gun?' Ellie asks Harvey then, and just before he can answer, I notice him shoot a look at Daryl.

'No, I don't,' he replies before loading up his plate with more fries and changing the subject to what the four of us might want to do tomorrow. But while he goes on about the potential for us to visit Santa Monica, I am wondering if he was honest when he said he didn't possess a firearm. I have no reason not to believe him, but there was something in the way he quickly looked at his son before he answered that makes me wonder if he was making sure Daryl didn't respond before him and give a different answer.

'What do you think, Dawn?' Harvey says to me, and I realise I've missed a little bit of the conversation during my daydream.

'What do I think?' I repeat, unsure.

'About tomorrow,' Harvey says with a smile. 'Anything you want to do?'

'Oh, erm. No, I'm not fussy. I'm happy to go with the flow.'

'Cool,' Harvey says before going back to his meal, and as we get to the point of finishing up with our food, I notice Ellie and Daryl yawning a little bit. But are they really both tired, or are they just wanting to excuse themselves from the table so they can be alone together?

Once again, as he seems to have done a number of times since I have been here, Harvey reads my mind and broaches the subject of tonight's sleeping arrangements for the four of us to discuss.

'Now, Dawn and I have been talking,' he begins as he looks at the couple across the table from us. 'And we have decided that we aren't going to be too old-fashioned and force the pair of you to sleep in separate bedrooms. I'm sure if we did, then you would only end up sneaking across the hallway in the middle of the night anyway. But we want the pair of you to be sensible and respectful. Remember this is a shared house and both your parents are present.'

Ellie and Daryl both seem embarrassed to have their parents thinking about such a thing and I'm confident Harvey couldn't have done a better job of making the whole thing between them feel less sexy by reminding them that we are present.

'Just try and get some sleep,' he says to Daryl and Ellie with a wink, one that I don't appreciate that much because I'm not sure I like the idea of him insinuating that they might be up all night doing something other than sleeping.

We've only just got here.

Is this going a little too fast?

Ellie and Daryl don't seem to think so because after yawning again, they say they are finished with their meals and stand up to take their empty plates into the kitchen.

'Don't worry about the tidying up. I'll do that,' Harvey says, and that's all the encouragement the pair need to leave the table to go and "chill out" elsewhere.

'Just one second, Ellie,' I say, and I get up from the table to go after her. 'I put my phone charger in your suitcase and just need to grab it. Can you give me a hand?'

Ellie looks confused, as she well might because I definitely did not put my phone charger in her suitcase, but I just needed an excuse to have a private moment with her, and once we are in her bedroom, I close the door so that Harvey and Daryl won't be able to hear what I'm about to say.

'Be sensible, Ellie,' I tell my daughter just after she asks me what I'm doing. 'I get that you're both adults, and you are free to make your own choices, but don't be rushed into anything if you're not ready. We're here for a week, so there's plenty of time if you want to take things slowly.'

'I'm fine,' Ellie says before rolling her eyes and groaning, as any child would do if their parent tried to talk to them about sex. But I'm not being a prude, nor am I naïve. I am sure my daughter has already slept with other people at her age, not that she would ever tell me much about that. But that's not the point. The point is that this is not a normal scenario.

'I know that you've been talking to Daryl for a while online,' I say as Ellie continues to pull her face. 'But that's not the same as getting to know him in person. So before you rush into anything, don't be afraid to talk a little more. Get to know him further, okay? And, of course, whatever you decide to do, take precautions.'

'Mum!'

Ellie has heard enough now and tries to push me out of her bedroom, but I've said everything I needed to say to her, so I allow myself to be bundled back out into the hallway. When I am, I spot Daryl lurking awkwardly outside his bedroom door and when he sees me, he smiles the shy smile of a young man who has to pretend he doesn't really want to have sex with my daughter.

It's too early for me to stay upstairs, not to mention it would be a little rude of me to do so because Harvey will have to do all the tidying up himself downstairs, so I go back down to find him, leaving Ellie and Daryl up above to get up to whatever they might wish to.

Relax, I think to myself as I return to the dining table to find Harvey clearing away the dirty plates. *Ellie is an adult, and she will make sensible choices.*

I just have to trust her.

Just like I'm having to trust Daryl and Harvey.

15

DAWN

Harvey and I have decided to deal with the awkwardness of what our children might be getting up to upstairs by pouring ourselves another alcoholic drink and taking a seat back out by the pool.

It's a lovely warm evening, and the sound of crickets fills the air as we sit by the calm water and sip our cold beverages as the sun sets on my first day in Southern California. But after a very, very long journey and with my body clock completely off kilter, I can't help but yawn a couple of times and when I do, I feel bad because it's a little rude to do such a thing in somebody else's company. But Harvey doesn't mind, although it seems he's not quite ready to let me go to bed yet based on what he says to me next.

'I hope you didn't mind me letting Ellie and Daryl know that they could share the same bed here,' he says as he nurses his cup of wine. 'I mean, I know we discussed it briefly earlier, but you hadn't actually said if you were okay with it or not. I should have double checked.'

'No, it's okay, honestly.'

'It's just that I know what it's like to sleep alone and wake up alone ever since, well, you know,' Harvey goes on. 'It's not much fun, right? And besides, sleeping in the same bed as somebody else doesn't just automatically mean it's all about sex. It's about other good things, too, like being close to another human being. Intimacy. Having the kinds of conversation that can only occur when two people are lying beside each other in the dead of night.'

Harvey looks sad then, most likely wistful for the time when he had somebody to lie beside and talk to and that somebody would be his late wife, who left him just as abruptly as Sean left me. Having seen a couple of photos of Jodie in the house earlier but not wanting to bring up the topic too soon, I figure this might be the right time to finally ask Harvey about the woman he used to be married to. After all, if we're going to be in each other's company for the next week while our kids keep sneaking away to be together, we're going to need all the conversation starters we can get or else risk a lot of silences before I'm due to fly home.

'How did you cope?' I ask him as I look down into the top of my cup. 'When you first lost Jodie, I mean.'

'Truthfully? I'm not sure I did,' Harvey replies with a heavy sigh. 'I drank too much, I slept too little and I ate terribly. You?'

'Same,' I confirm with a sad shrug. 'I'm not sure how I survived when I look back on it.'

'Me neither. I guess I kept going for Daryl, just like you did for Ellie. But it wasn't easy, and it's still not easy now.'

While this is not the first time that I've been around another grieving spouse since I lost Sean, this is the first time I actually feel ready to really talk about it. That's because the group therapy sessions I went to back home came far too soon for me, and since then, I've only really opened up to my friends, who are always sympathetic but have thankfully never been through what I have.

'The nights are definitely the hardest,' I admit. 'You can stay busy up to a certain point in the daytime so that you don't really have time to think about it. But it's at night when everything quietens down that I find it tough. I suppose that's why I started taking on some night shifts where I work.'

'Weekends are hard too,' Harvey says ruefully. 'The majority of the week isn't so bad when you think everyone is busy working. But at the weekend, that's the time when families and friends get together. It's the social time. But it's not much fun when you don't have your best friend there with you to socialise with.'

If my heart wasn't already broken, then it would be breaking now for the man sitting beside me by this pool but instead, we're just two damaged people sharing a drink as the sky gets increasingly darker above our heads.

'I miss her every day, and I know I always will,' Harvey says, and not for the first time since I got here, I note the absence of the wedding ring on his hand. He notices me looking then and chooses to acknowledge it.

'I stopped wearing it a couple of months ago,' he tells me. 'I didn't want to take it off, but it was just a constant reminder of her that I was carrying around with me everywhere, so I figured it might be easier if I just stopped seeing it every day.'

'I understand,' I say, though it's obvious I have not come to the same conclusion as him by the fact that I

am still very much wearing my ring, a fact that isn't lost on Harvey.
'I suppose I have to try and move on at some point,' he says as he rubs the spot on his finger where his wedding band once was. 'And I guess it would be pretty awkward to be going on dates with a new woman whilst wearing a wedding ring. It might confuse the other person a little.'
We laugh then, and it's a welcome moment of brevity after a sombre period.
'So you think you're ready to try and meet someone new?' I ask him as the wind rustles in the palm trees over by the garden fence.
'I don't know. I mean, I think I should try. Either that or spend the rest of my life by myself,' Harvey says with a shrug. 'Daryl won't be living here forever and then it'll just be me pottering around this place. It's a nice house, but I can't imagine it'll be much fun if I'm alone all the time.'
'I guess it just depends on what feels right to you.'
'I guess. What about you?'
'What about me?' I ask, far more comfortable asking the questions than fielding them.
'Are you ready to meet someone new?'
'Dating? No way. I don't think so.'
'Too soon?'
'Yeah. I mean, no. I mean, I'm not sure. It's just-'
'Don't worry, it was just a question. You don't have to explain anything to me.'
'No, it's okay,' I say, aware that talking this through might be beneficial to me somewhere down the line. 'I guess I'll never be able to say that I've truly moved on

unless I give myself the chance to fall in love with somebody else. Maybe if I was much older, then I wouldn't see the point and could be happy enough by myself in old age. But just like Daryl and you, Ellie won't be living at home forever, and I don't like the thought of being by myself for the next thirty or forty years.'

A silence falls between us then, and as we share a look, we hold each other's gazes for a moment. As we do, I sense something between us. That's why I suddenly snap out of it and put my drink down on the table before saying I really need to call it a night.

'Sleep well,' Harvey says to me with that warm, compassionate smile he wears so well as I get up to go inside the house, and I thank him for his lovely hospitality so far before bidding him goodnight.

The cool air-con is a relief to my flushed face as I make my way through the house and head upstairs, but I know it's not the Rosé that has caused my cheeks to redden.

Did Harvey and I just have a moment out there by the pool?

If so, then not only is that a little awkward, but it would be entirely inappropriate. Our children are dating each other, so nothing can happen between us, not that I would want it to anyway. This trip is all about Ellie and Daryl and their budding romance, not their grieving parents who haven't been loved by anyone themselves in a long time. Who knows what the future holds for our kids? Ellie and Daryl may end up getting married one day and that would mean I'm related to Harvey. That's why we can't do anything that could make that weird.

So, no more sharing long looks.
Maybe even no more late-night heart-to-hearts with a bottle of alcohol.
And certainly, under no circumstances must the two of us ever get close enough to kiss.
I feel a little out of breath as I close my bedroom door and lean back against it, looking at my suitcase on the bed as I do and thinking about how all of this is just me being silly. It's a consequence of my tired, sleep-deprived mind. I just need a good night's rest and to allow my body to adjust to American time. Then I'll realise that Harvey and I are just two people who can be friends because our children are in love with each other. At that point, I'll stop allowing myself to think about his nice smile or his handsome face and the fact that he has already got me to open up more about my grief in the last few hours than anybody else has in the last few years, a fact that must mean I have already formed a connection with this man that runs quite deep.
I will forget about all those things.
Right?

16

ELLIE

I've been dreaming about it for so long and now it's actually happened. Daryl and I have slept together, and it was perfect! I was so nervous and I think he was too, but that's okay because it's cute. We took things slowly, not because Mum told us to, but because that was just the right pace for us. But once we started, things got pretty fast, real quick.

He's such a good kisser. Much better than anyone else I've ever kissed before. But I knew he would be. I could tell. I've always known he was nothing like the other guys in my past and he has proven it tonight.

It was weird knowing that our parents were downstairs, but we didn't have much choice. At least they didn't make us sleep in separate rooms, although Mum seemed to be unsure about that. But this was always going to happen because I didn't just come here to talk to Daryl. I came here to get closer to him and now that I have, things are even more special.

I can't wipe the smile off my face as I sit and write my diary, guided only by the light from my mobile phone. Otherwise, the room is dark and that's because the sun hasn't come up yet outside. I've been wide awake since 3 am thanks to jet lag, but rather than lie here and be bored or wake Daryl up, I've decided to update my diary.

This is my first entry since we landed in America, and I've had a lot to say. I've written about how it felt to finally meet Daryl properly and actually touch him and look into his eyes. I've also written about his dad and how he seems really nice. One thing I couldn't not mention was the house they live in because it's amazing, and I'm sure it won't be the last time I write about that swimming pool in this diary. But now I've got onto the really good stuff. Daryl and I have 'done it', and it was so good that I can't wait for him to wake up so that we can do it again. But he's fast asleep at the moment, no jet lag for him, so I'll let him rest and just keep writing instead.

I guess it's always a big worry when you meet someone you like and wonder what it will be like to be physical with them. It would be great to say that it's not important and all that matters is the conversation or how you feel just to be near them. But that wouldn't be telling the truth. For everything to be perfect with Daryl, the sex had to be great too and it was!

So now what? He's ticked every box I would have for a potential boyfriend. He's kind, funny, sensitive, hard-working, but I already knew all that before I got here. The only thing I didn't know was what he would be like when he was holding me in his arms and our lips were about to meet. But now I know, what does this mean for our future? I can't think of a single reason why I wouldn't want to be with Daryl more. He's everything I've ever wanted in a man, and now that we're here together in the same bed, I never want to leave him.

How can I go back to England and be apart from him when I know we are so right for each other? That would just be stupid. We're meant to be together and now that we are, I'm not letting this go. I want this to work, but it can only do that if we don't have to go back to doing the long-distance thing. That means one of us has to move to be with the other one.

Me or him.

We talked about it a little bit before we went to sleep, and while Daryl said he was willing to go anywhere to be with me, he did talk about how he had plans for his job over here and would be able to find work easily. As for me, I could just get a waitress job anywhere, so why not do that over here? There would be no point me dragging Daryl to England when I could easily just move here. And why wouldn't I? This weather is amazing, and he has a pool! Okay, so it's his dad's house, but we could get our own place one day with our own pool, and how cool would that be! My friends back home would be so jealous! Sure, I'd miss them, but they could fly out and see me. A girl's holiday in LA, except for me, it wouldn't be a holiday. It would be my everyday life. What a place to live.

But what about Mum?

I stop writing as I consider the one potential obstacle in all of this. There's no way Mum will want me to move here permanently. I'd have to marry Daryl to get a visa, which I'm sure I could do, but Mum wouldn't want me to live so far away from home. I get it because me being here would mean her being by herself back in England. I'd miss her as much as she missed me. But

what am I supposed to do? Sacrifice my future happiness to stay near her?
I have to live my own life at some point, right?

While it's a very awkward subject to tackle with Mum, it is a problem I can kick a little further down the road into the future because I don't have to talk about it with her straight away. But I will do soon, maybe even as early as next week when we're due to fly home.

Am I even going to be getting on that plane with her?

There's movement in the bed beside me then, and I realise Daryl is awake as he rolls over to look at me.

'You okay?' he asks me as he notices my diary and the torchlight on my phone through his squinting, sleepy eyes.

'Sorry, did I wake you?' I ask, quickly turning off the light and plunging the bedroom back into darkness again. 'I just couldn't sleep. Damn jet lag.'

'What time is it in England right now?'

'Nearly midday.'

'Ouch. That'll be why you're wide awake.'

'Yeah.'

I put my diary down and snuggle into Daryl's warm body, a smile on my face that more than masks my level of sleep deprivation. I smile even more when I feel him kiss the top of my head, and while I still feel far too awake to get any more sleep, I would be more than happy just to lie here like this for the next few hours until sunrise.

But it seems Daryl has other plans.

'Do you want to go on an adventure?' he asks me as I listen to the beating of his heart through his chest.

'What?'

'There's somewhere I want to take you. Do you want to go now?'

'It's the middle of the night.'

'I know, but we need to get there before the sun comes up for it to be worth it.'

I sit up a little then as Daryl turns on a bedside lamp, allowing us to see each other properly.

'What are you talking about?' I ask.

'There's this place I go to sometimes that has the most amazing views, and the sunrise from there is incredible. Shall we go?'

'Where is it?'

'Not far. I could drive us.'

Daryl's smile almost persuades me to say yes without giving it any more thought, but then a small voice of reason speaks up in my mind, reminding me that it might not be a great idea to get up while others in the house are still sleeping.

'It's too early,' I say, but Daryl just shrugs and pulls back the duvet before getting up and starting to get dressed.

'It's fine. We'll be quiet. We won't wake anybody. Come on, let's go.'

I'm still a little unsure, but as Daryl puts on his clothes, I figure he wouldn't want to be taking me to wherever we are going if it wasn't worth seeing. Maybe he's been planning this for when I get here. It could be some big romantic gesture. If so, then I don't want to ruin it, so that's why I get out of bed as well, and a few minutes later, we're both dressed and creeping out of the bedroom.

Daryl puts his fingers to his lips as he opens the door before we move out into the dark hallway, passing the bedroom door behind which Mum is sleeping and then going down the stairs to where Daryl carefully takes his car keys from the hook in the kitchen.

'Let's go,' he whispers to me as he leads me to the back door, and then, just like that, we are out of the house and standing outside in the chilly darkness. But it won't stay cold or dark for long, not when the sun comes up in a few hours. And when it does, Daryl and I are going to have the best view of it in the city.

17

DAWN

Something just woke me up. Was it jet lag? This unfamiliar and slightly uncomfortable bed? Or was it the sound of a car engine starting outside?

I listen out for any more noises, but I don't hear anything, so I close my eyes and try to get back to sleep. I know from just opening them then that it's still dark outside, so I don't want to be awake yet. But the problem is I've been disturbed now, and despite my best efforts, I can't drop off into slumber again easily.

Letting out a frustrated sigh, I roll onto my back and stare at the ceiling of this strange bedroom I have found myself in, thousands of miles away from my own. Despite managing to get some rest, it still doesn't change the fact that it feels weird to be here.

I wonder how Ellie has slept. *If she has slept at all.* But best not to dwell on that too much, so I roll over and close my eyes again.

Another frustrating period passes before I give up on sleep altogether and decide that I need a drink. Unfortunately, I didn't possess the foresight to bring a glass up to bed with me, so I'm going to have to go downstairs to the kitchen to get one. But that's okay because one of the many things Harvey told me when he was giving me the rundown of what it will be like to stay here as a guest was that he doesn't turn on the house alarm at night, so I don't have to worry about activating that if I get up at some point. I guess that is another perk of living in a safe neighbourhood, but I'm still trying to be as quiet as possible as I leave my bedroom and go downstairs because I'd hate to be that annoying guest who sleeps over and wakes up the host. Harvey might like me so far but I bet the novelty of me being here would wear off pretty fast if I kept disturbing his slumber for the duration of my stay.

Making it downstairs without so much as stepping on a creaky floorboard, because I'm not sure this house possesses anything that old, I enter the kitchen and go in search of a glass. It's not easy to find what you need in somebody else's cupboards, though, so it takes me a while before I get what I want and make my way over to the tap.

Once my glass is full, I take a large gulp of cool water and while it's refreshing, it also does the annoying job of waking me up a little more, and I'm well aware that it will be pointless for me to go back to bed now.

I'm up, but it's still the middle of the night.

So what should I do now?

I guess the obvious thing to do is the same thing I'd do if I woke up in the middle of the night at home and that is to go and watch television for a little while. I have no idea what might be on at this time, but there's bound to be some early-morning American talk show starting soon, right?

I'm just about to leave the kitchen to go and find the TV when I notice the closed door by the fridge. I saw it earlier but have no idea what the door might lead to because going through it was not a part of the guided tour that Harvey took me on earlier. Maybe that's just because it's simply a storage cupboard and there's nothing exciting to see in there. Or maybe it's a utility room with a washing machine and some old household items, which again, would not be particularly interesting. But I'm curious enough to go and have a quick look for myself, so I approach the door, and as I turn the handle, I am almost hoping that I'm going to find some tasty snacks hidden behind here that I could perhaps treat myself to while I watch TV. Harvey did tell me to make myself at home after all. But then I open the door and see that it's not a place where food is stored, nor is it a room for utility items.

All I see is a set of steps leading down to what I presume must be the basement.

It looks very dark down there, so my first thought is to close this door again and stay up here. But I wonder what could be down there. I also wonder why Harvey didn't tell me there was a basement here. I doubt he's hiding anything but considering how eager he was to show me everything when I got here, there must be a reason why he deemed this the one part of the house that should stay secret.

Reaching around for a light switch, I manage to find a cable hanging down and when I pull it, a small lightbulb turns on at the foot of the stairs. That allows me to see just how deep the basement is below this house, as well as what the room contains.

It's not that deep, only six or seven steps down, but it certainly contains a lot. I can see numerous cardboard boxes down there, some of them piled on top of each other while a few sit alone and a few are open as if they have recently been accessed.

Meh. It's a basement full of old things. Turn the light off now, close this door and go and watch TV.

That's what I tell myself.

But that's not what I do.

I creep down the stairs, careful because my bare feet are now treading over dusty wooden steps, and I don't want to stand on a nail or anything like that. But when I get to the bottom, I can see a little more.

Or at least I can see more boxes.

I guess this is where Harvey stores all his mostly unused or unwanted things. Much like my attic at home, this seems to be the place he has chosen to hide away all the things that he's not yet gotten around to throwing away. My attic is full of old photographs, paperwork, books, and toys from when Ellie was young, and I guess all these boxes are full of similar things. No wonder Harvey didn't take me down here earlier. He's probably ashamed at how much clutter he has managed to accumulate in his lifetime and didn't want me to think he was some kind of hoarder.

Approaching the nearest box, I peer inside, expecting to see some miscellaneous documents or unused photo frames or something of that fairly mundane nature. But what I actually see are several pairs of women's shoes.

Taking out a stylish black boot, I admire it for a moment before putting it back and opening a second box. In there, I find a pair of faded jeans and a couple of blouses, neatly folded and just as stylish as the shoes. That's when I realise what this stuff must be.

It must have all belonged to Jodie.
And Harvey hasn't been able to bring himself to throw it all away yet.
A wave of sorrow washes over me as I check a couple more boxes and confirm my theory. Yes, these are all Jodie's possessions, no longer in use now she has passed away but still in this house because I guess that's where they belong. But instead of being in the wardrobes upstairs, taking up space in the bedroom she shared with her husband, they are now down here, resigned to this dark, dusty basement, and all because life is unfair and unpredictable.
I decide it would be disrespectful to touch any more of these things now I know what these boxes contain, so I go to leave the basement but as I do, I accidentally knock over a box behind me, spilling the contents all over the floor.
'Oh no,' I say, terrified that somebody upstairs would have heard that and hating the idea of Harvey coming down here to find me disrupting all the memories he has of his wife.
Kneeling down, I begin trying to get the items back in the box, items that mostly consist of paperwork and photos. I see a couple of images of Jodie with Harvey and Daryl and drop them back into the box carefully but quickly, but then I pick up a photo showing a woman who isn't her.
The woman in this photograph is much younger, early twenties, I'd say, with dark hair and a pretty smile as she stands beside Daryl, who has his arm around her. Is this a friend of his or an ex-girlfriend? If so, better that I saw

it rather than Ellie. But the more I look, the more I recognise her from somewhere, though I can't quite place it.

Then it hits me.

This is the young woman in the missing person poster I saw on the way here from the airport.

It's Aubree.

So Daryl knew her? That must mean Harvey did too. But if so, why didn't he say anything when I asked him about the poster in the car?

Was he close to her and if so, was it too upsetting for him to mention?

Or was there some other reason he didn't say that he and his son knew her?

Do they know what happened to her?

I don't know the answers to any of those questions, but I know this is something I will want to mention to Ellie the next time I'm alone with her but to do that, I'll need proof. That's why I take a picture of the photograph with my phone so I can show it to her later. But no sooner have I done that than I'm startled by a noise at the top of the stairs, and as I turn around, I see Harvey coming down into the basement towards me.

'What are you doing?' he asks me just after I've put my phone away out of sight.

'Nothing!' I say, far too quickly for it to seem innocent, and despite trying to put the photos away and return the box to its upright position, it's futile because Harvey has seen me and knows now that I've been snooping.

Should I ask him about the woman in the photo with Daryl?

Or would it be safer to just leave it?

I make a snap decision not to say anything because while I'm sure there is nothing sinister to this, better to play it safe and not question Harvey about a potentially dangerous subject when he has me cornered down here in his basement.

'Sorry. I couldn't sleep. I wasn't prying, I just got lost and accidentally knocked a box over.'

I try to leave then, hoping to pass Harvey and get up the stairs now that I've put everything back where it belongs down here. But that's when he steps across me and blocks my exit route, and suddenly, I feel afraid of this man.

'What are you doing?' I ask him, looking up at him as he stares down at me with a serious expression on his face. But he doesn't say anything, so I try to get past him again, only this time, he puts his hands up and holds onto my arms.

Maybe it's my fatigue that's increasing my paranoia but I panic then and do the only thing I can do and that is to call out to Ellie, hoping that I will wake her up and she will come downstairs to help me. But when I do, Harvey just shakes his head.

'Save your breath,' he says in a cold tone. 'She's gone.'

18

ELLIE

The sky is still completely black as Daryl drives us out of the city, and I stifle another yawn as I sit in the passenger seat and wonder where we are going.

'How long until we get there?' I ask, hoping I don't sound too much like an annoying child with that question, but I am eager to know, not because I'm worried, just curious.

'Not long,' Daryl replies before he takes one hand off the wheel and turns on the radio.

A country song plays first, but he fiddles around with the dial until he finds something a little more suited to our tastes, and as the bass from a more upbeat track comes out of the speakers, Daryl gives me a grin and goes back to concentrating on the road.

His hands drum the steering wheel of his car, the one he told me his dad bought him for his twenty-first birthday. It's not the most glamorous vehicle I've ever seen, and the interior could certainly do with a good clean, but Daryl seems happy enough with it and why wouldn't he be? At our age, we don't care what we drive, we just care that we are able to.

I recline my seat a little before kicking off my shoes and putting my feet up on the dashboard, and Daryl doesn't seem to mind that because I'm clearly relaxing and enjoying the drive now. I suspect he's glad that I've stopped bothering him with questions about where we are going and when we will get there. All I know is that it has something to do with the impending sunrise, so I'm guessing he is taking me to some vantage point from which we can see the sun come up over the city.

What's that place I've seen in the movies, the one where the characters go and overlook Los Angeles with the skyscrapers in the distance and the Hollywood sign on a hill nearby? The Griffith Observatory? Is that where we are going? It could be but I don't want to say that to Daryl in case I guess right and ruin his big surprise. If not there, then I guess we're going to somewhere similar.

Somewhere high up.

Somewhere we can see everything.

Somewhere we can be alone.

I can't predict exactly how this morning is going to go because we're not there yet, but just the fact that Daryl is trying to do something romantic for me only puts him even further ahead of all the other boys from my past. None of them tried to do anything particularly nice for me. No flowers, no chocolates and certainly no scenic sunsets. They were just happy enough to try and get me drunk so I might do a little more than give them a kiss, and based on what my friends told me, that was what all their boyfriends were like too. But once again, Daryl is not only surpassing my admittedly low expectations for men, but making it even more impossible to imagine meeting somebody else who might be better than him.

As we cruise on through the dark, empty streets, I have an idea and take out my phone. It's midday back home, so all my friends will be awake and that means they will see if I was to share something on social media now. Aware that I haven't put anything online yet to document my trip, I decide to film a short video of myself in the car with Daryl to upload to Instagram, one that is sure to make everybody who follows me back home very envious that I'm out here having fun in LA while they are in the middle of another boring day in the UK.

I snap a couple of photos out of the window before starting to record, moving my phone around the car before making sure the camera picks up Daryl at the wheel.

'What are you doing?' he asks me, his eyes diverting from the road ahead to the device I'm holding near his face.

'Just making something for my Instagram,' I say before I stop recording and check the video. Happy with it, I begin typing out a caption to accompany it, deciding that *'Cruising around Cali at 4am'* is good enough to do the job. But just before I can upload it, Daryl voices an objection.

'Don't put it online if I'm in it,' he says, suddenly sounding very shy, which is weird because he's never seemed like that to me before.

'What? Why?'

'I just don't like it. I'm not a big social media guy.'

'But it's not going on your account, it's going on mine.'

'So? People will still see it.'

'Yeah, that's the idea of social media,' I jest.

'I don't want you to put it on.'

'Why not?'

'I just don't.'

I'm very confused now, but Daryl just turns to me and smiles.

'Sorry. It's nice that you want to put things online about what we are getting up to, but there'll be lots of chances to do that when we go to the beach. But this is just a private thing for me and you. Can we keep it that way?'

'A private thing?'

'Yeah, just for the two of us. We don't have to share everything with the world, do we?'

'I guess not.'

'How about we take a nice photo when we get there, and you can put that online?'

'Okay. But I could just put this video on as well. I think it's cool.'

'We'll get something much better than that when we get there, don't worry.'

Daryl gives me a wink before turning off the road we're on, and I see then that we are entering the freeway.

'How far away is this place?' I ask again.

'Just outside the city,' Daryl says.

'That sounds far.'

'It's not that far.'

Daryl increases our speed then, and as we zoom along the quiet freeway, I think about what Mum might think if she wakes up and finds out I've gone off somewhere secretly, somewhere a long way from where I'm supposed to be.

'It's a good thing we're doing this early,' Daryl says, his foot still down on the accelerator pedal and the speedometer creeping towards 100. 'This freeway will be completely jammed in a couple of hours when everybody starts going to work.'

That might be the case, but we have the road to ourselves now, and that's why it doesn't take long for us to leave the city behind, the bright lights twinkling far behind us as the buildings become sparser, and now we appear to be entering the desert.

I can just about make out the tops of some of the mountains in the distance through the eerie gloom as we whizz along a straight stretch of tarmac that leads out into what looks like a completely barren wilderness. It's crazy to think that one minute ago we were surrounded by concrete and big houses, and now there is nothing other than vast empty spaces on the other side of my window.

It's then that I realise I couldn't upload anything to social media even if I still wanted to because I no longer have a phone signal, and while the radio still seems to be working, my phone is now effectively useless.

'How much further?' I ask Daryl as we go at a fast enough speed to make me take my feet off the dashboard and sit up a little straighter, just in case we have to suddenly hit the brakes.

'Not far,' Daryl replies before turning up the song on the radio. 'Just sit back and relax.'

He goes back to drumming his hands on the steering wheel then and by the looks of things, he's completely chilled out. So why aren't I? Why can't I just do as he says and relax?

Why am I worried?

This is supposed to be an adventure, right? A fun little road trip with my boyfriend. A journey into the wilds of America. This is the kind of excitement I was craving back when I was working as a waitress in that rubbish restaurant in my hometown.

So why am I not excited now?

Is it because I've suddenly realised that I'm headed into the middle of nowhere with a guy I don't know quite as well as I like to think I do?

And is it because I know my mum would freak the hell out if she knew I'd allowed myself to be put into a potentially risky situation like this without telling her where I was going?

19

DAWN

'Where is my daughter?'

It should be a simple enough question but the man who has been asked it is not answering me. Harvey is still just standing in front of me, blocking my exit from this basement, the same basement in which I just saw a photo showing his son and that missing woman who no one seems to know what happened to.

'Harvey! What is going on?'

I'm getting distressed now, but that realisation seems to be the trigger for Harvey to speak again and when he does, he surprises me.

'I have no idea. I just woke up and saw Daryl's car had gone.'

'What?'

'I woke up to go to the bathroom. I never sleep well after drinking too much wine. But when I looked outside, I saw Daryl's car was not on the driveway. I went to check his room and found the bed empty. Then I went to find you, but you were gone as well.'

Is he telling me the truth?

'They've both gone?' I ask.

'Yes, it seems so.'

'But it's the middle of the night!'

'I know, I'm not happy about this either.'

'What is your son doing with my daughter?'

My question is a very accusatory one but based on the photo I just saw and now being aware of Daryl's link to Aubree, I am already fearing the worst.
What if Daryl hurt her, and what if he is about to do the same thing to Ellie?

'Calm down, I'm sure they're both fine,' Harvey says breezily. 'They probably couldn't sleep so just went for a drive.'

'A drive?'

'Yeah, Daryl is probably showing Ellie some of the sights. The roads are quiet at this time, so they might have gone further into the city.'

'No, Ellie wouldn't just go out without telling me.'

'Wouldn't she? Daryl does that all the time.'

'I don't care what your son does, I just want to know that Ellie is okay!'

'She'll be fine!'

'How do you know that?'

I glare at Harvey, but he doesn't have an answer for me there.

'We need to go and find them now,' I say forcefully, and I head for the stairs again. Thankfully, this time, Harvey does not try and stop me, and as I leave the basement, I feel relieved to be back out of the claustrophobic room full of boxes of his late wife's things. But it's the photo of Aubree that is still on my mind the most as I step back into the kitchen, and I consider mentioning it to Harvey as he joins me.

But what if it's a mistake to do so? What if he and his son have something to hide? If so, they might do anything to keep me quiet, and then I'll never be able to help Ellie get out of whatever situation she might be in now. That's why I decide not to mention it just yet and, instead, see if I can get through to Ellie on her phone.

'I'm going to call her,' I say to Harvey, and he tells me he's going to try Daryl's mobile as well. I don't know if he's being truthful or not, but he did seem genuinely surprised when he was telling me about waking up to find our children had snuck out so maybe he is on my side here.

I find Ellie's number on my device and call, praying that she will answer me and let me know that she is okay. Hopefully, she's nearby and is not involved in anything more dramatic than a quick visit to a 24/7 convenience store to pick up a few snacks before coming back to the house. If so, maybe I don't need to worry anymore. But until I know she is okay, then I am going to worry lots because at present, my daughter is missing in a foreign land with a man who may not be who he seems.

But no sooner have I tried to call Ellie than I hear an automated voice at the other end of the line telling me that connecting my call is not possible unless I upgrade my tariff.

Damn my network and its rules about international calls!

Needing a Plan B quickly, I ask Harvey if I can use his phone to call Ellie. He says I can and happily hands his device to me, but it comes with a warning.

'Good luck. I just tried Daryl, and either his phone is turned off or he has no signal.'

That doesn't sound promising, but I have a go anyway, typing Ellie's number into Harvey's mobile before trying her. But just like with Daryl, I can't get through.

'Your call cannot be connected,' says the voice at the other end of the line, a message that does nothing to calm my jangling nerves, and now, with no way of contacting Ellie, I have no idea how I am supposed to figure out where she is and if she is okay.

'Relax, I'm sure they're fine,' Harvey says, no doubt having spotted the angst written all over my face.

'I want to know where he has taken her,' I say, not in the mood to be told to calm down because Harvey is not the one in a strange country trying to find his missing child. He might be calm because Daryl knows this area well. But Ellie doesn't. She isn't from here. LA is not her home, nor is it mine.

We are so far out of our comfort zone here that 'relaxing' is just not going to happen.

'I guess we're both up now, so how about some coffee?' Harvey suggests as if this is just a typical morning. But it's far from it, and I make that clear by telling him I don't give a damn about coffee, and that seems to be the thing that finally makes him realise just how stressed out I am.

'Look, I get it. You've got separation anxiety with Ellie,' he says as if he has me all figured out. 'I used to get the same thing with Daryl. It's just another one of the many things I had to go through after losing my wife, and I suppose it's the same for you. But just because something bad happened to your partner, it doesn't mean something bad is going to happen to your child too. You can't be with them all the time, and you can't follow them everywhere, certainly not at their age. You just have to trust that everything will be okay.'

Everything will be okay? Is that really what I am supposed to believe in?

'It's not separation anxiety,' I tell Harvey, dismissing that notion as quickly as I've dismissed his last piece of advice to me. 'This has nothing to do with losing my husband and everything to do with wanting to make sure that my daughter is safe on her first day in a foreign country with a boy she has only just met.'

'So what's the problem? You don't trust my son with your daughter?' Harvey asks me, suddenly getting a little too close to the crux of the matter. 'Is this more about a problem you have with him and maybe me rather than Ellie?'

'I didn't say that.'

'But that's how it looks.'

I could just be honest and say that yes, I have my reservations about Daryl, but I have a feeling that is not going to be the thing that persuades Harvey to help me look for them any quicker, so I don't confirm it. Instead, I try another tactic.

'You're right,' I say, allowing a little more emotion to come to the surface so that Harvey can see just how afraid I am. 'It is separation anxiety, and I know it's something I need to deal with at some point. But right now, please can you just help me? Is there anywhere you can think of that Daryl might have driven Ellie to?'

I look at Harvey with hope and a few tears in my eyes and the more I do, the more he seems to do what I say and think. Then suddenly, he has something.

'There is one place he might have taken her,' he says as he runs a hand over the stubble on his chiselled chin. 'It might be a bit of a long shot, but I know he has been there before, and it might explain why neither of them have a phone signal at the moment.'

'Where is it?' I ask, ready to go now, although that's clearly not the case because neither of us are properly dressed to go outside, a fact Harvey already seems to be aware of.

'Put some warmer clothes on,' he tells me as he turns for the stairs. 'It'll be chilly out there until the sun comes up.'

I hurry away to do as he says, and once we are both dressed and ready to hit the road, I hope he is right about where he thinks Daryl and Ellie might have gone.

'Get in the car. I'll just lock up,' Harvey tells me as he pushes the button on his key fob to unlock his vehicle, and as I get in the passenger side, Harvey closes the front door and puts the key in the lock.

Full of nervous tension and unable to sit still, my knees bounce up and down, my restless legs eager to be on the move to find my daughter. But as I do that, I accidentally nudge the glove compartment in front of me, and it falls open.

Going to shut it before Harvey gets in the car, I freeze when I see what is lying inside the compartment on top of a small stack of paperwork.

It's a gun.

The very thing that Harvey told me earlier that he did not possess.

20

ELLIE

The desolate landscape that I can just about make out in the darkness on the other side of the car window is showing no sign of becoming any less sparse and unpopulated as Daryl drives us on further and further away from the city. Several more checks on my phone confirm what I already knew, which is that I still have no phone signal and am, therefore, entirely uncontactable or unable to contact anybody myself. I just hope that Mum is still asleep, otherwise I just know she will be worrying about me, and that anxiety will only grow if she can't reach me on my mobile.

I don't want her to worry for many reasons, not least because I don't want her to have any excuse to decide that me moving here permanently is a bad idea. But if I'm a little worried about this situation, then I know she definitely will be, so all I can hope is that she is still entirely oblivious to it.

'Is everything okay?' I ask Daryl as he continues to take us further into the desert.

'Huh? Of course. Why wouldn't it be?'

'We're really far away from the city.'

'So?'

'I just don't know where we're going.'

'It's a surprise like I told you. But don't worry, we're almost there now.'

With that, Daryl indicates to come off the quiet highway, and after slowing, he turns us onto a smaller road that leads towards one of the many mountains that seem to surround us on almost every side now.

The car judders as the tyres rumble over the rougher surface after we have swapped the smooth tarmac for this stone-speckled dirt track, but I'm still wary about where we might be going because this seems to be even more remote than where we were a minute ago. At least on the main highway, there was a chance of seeing another driver. But here, on this road, that seems very unlikely, and the headlights from this car are the only thing for miles around.

Don't be silly, I tell myself when a scary thought flashes through my mind. It's one in which I briefly entertain the idea of Daryl being some kind of serial killer who has driven me out into the middle of nowhere to kill me and bury me in the desert. Then, after I've been missing for a while, my photo will appear on both the American and the UK news channels, and I'll become a famous missing person, getting international attention before everybody gets bored of the mystery and moves on when my body has failed to be found anywhere.

Is that my fate? Will all my friends back home be reading about me online and speculating about what happened to me? And will Mum be forced to spend the rest of her life out here, searching this desert for any sign of me while Daryl smugly sits in a prison cell and refuses to tell her what he did to her daughter?

I need some fresh air, but with Daryl still driving, the only way I can get it is to lower my window a little. When I do, the noise of the air rushing into the vehicle is loud, but it makes me feel a tiny bit better. Daryl has noticed what I've done, but he just smiles at me before concentrating on the road again and when I do the same, I see that the track ahead of us has an incline to it now.

We're heading up a little higher, following a pathway carved into the side of this particular mountain, and the more we go up, the more I wonder how many people have been up here before me.

Is this a tourist place? If so, I would feel much better about this. But it's still early and dark, and with no one else around, I can't be sure that everything is okay here.

The beam from the headlights bounces off several rocky surfaces, showing me the edges of red rocks that have no doubt stood for a very long time. But I'm here now, so I only care about what happens next, not what happened millions of years ago to form this striking landscape. Fortunately, it looks like I'm about to find out because after taking us higher and higher, Daryl finally brings the car to a stop and turns off the engine.

'We're here,' he says with a smile, though quite where 'here' is is not clear because I can't see much of anything outside. 'Come on.'

Daryl gets out of the car then, so I guess I better do the same.

Following him out, I see he is already making his way up a path that cuts between two boulders, and while I hesitate for a moment, he turns back and gives me a wave to hurry up.

'Quick, we need to get there in time,' he tells me before slipping between the two boulders, and once he's through, I lose sight of him for a moment. But suddenly being alone in this eerily quiet place is not a nice feeling, so I scurry up the path, passing the boulders before I see Daryl standing on the edge of a clifftop. It's only as I get closer that I see just how far the drop is below us, so I take a couple of steps back, but Daryl has no such worries, and he takes a seat on the edge, allowing his legs to dangle over the side before he pats the ground beside him.

'Take a seat, the show is just about to begin,' he says as he checks his watch, but I'm still apprehensive about getting so close to the edge.

Daryl realises that because he quickly holds out his hand towards me, inviting me to come closer and trying to show me that there is nothing to be afraid of.

But isn't there?

What if I was to fall over the edge?

Or what if Daryl was to push me?

Almost embarrassed by the complete lack of trust I seem to be showing in my boyfriend, I tell myself that he loves me and would never hurt me, before taking a step forward and holding his hand and once I do that, Daryl leads me carefully to the edge before he helps me sit down. Then, once we're both in position on the clifftop, our legs swinging freely in the air below us, Daryl points into the distance over the vast, sprawling desert that lies before us.

'Watch this,' he says.

When I look up, I see the faintest glimmer of light appear on the horizon, but the more I watch, the more colour I see. It starts as a dark red, but it soon turns into a brighter orange, and then suddenly, it's yellow as the sun rises higher and higher and floods these great plains with beautiful, brilliant light.

Only then do I understand what Daryl has done for me.

He has brought me all the way out here to witness this.

A magnificent, majestic sunrise that I'll never forget.

With his arm around me, Daryl asks me what I think, but I almost have no words to give him because I am blown away by the spectacular light show going on right in front of us. But when I do turn to look at Daryl, he quickly leans in to give me a kiss, and as our faces are warmed by the increasing sunlight, the pair of us lock lips in what is easily the most romantic moment of my entire life.

'This is incredible,' I say after we have stopped kissing, and as I am able to see more and more things around me in the increasing light, I feel so foolish for ever being afraid that Daryl was taking me somewhere dangerous. He loves me, and he has only made that even clearer by making this romantic gesture for me.

'How did you find this place?' I ask him as we look up to see a large bird circling above our heads, the only other living thing besides us that I've seen out here since we left the city.

'This place is special to me,' Daryl says, his arm still wrapped around my shoulder. 'After Mum died, I just woke up early one morning and needed to get out of the house, so I started driving and ended up here. Next thing

I knew, the sun was coming up, and I saw the most amazing sunrise. Ever since then, I try to come back here as often as I can.'

It's a touching story and yet another insight into how Daryl struggled with the loss of his mother, but as the pair of us sit and bask in the warm glow of a new day, I have another question.

'Have you brought any other girls up here before me?'

I'm not asking it in a jealous way, more of a teasing way, but also as a little test because I am curious as to whether or not Daryl has shared this special place with anyone else or if he has saved it for someone he truly loves - that being me, of course. But Daryl shifts awkwardly then and removes his arm from around my shoulder before scoffing and saying no.

'You're the first,' he replies, but it's not very convincing, although maybe he's just being a little shy now because he doesn't want to admit that he has brought someone else here before me. But so what if he has? We both have our past relationships, and we have nothing to be ashamed of there, right?

But my question seems to have spoilt the mood somewhat, although maybe it's not such a big deal because the sun is up now, so I guess the show is over, meaning it's time for us to head back before our parents wake up and find out we sneaked away.

'I guess we better go back to the car,' I say after a quiet moment in which the only sound was from that same bird squawking up in the pale blue sky above our heads. But Daryl says there is no rush, before telling me to relax and enjoy the scenery for a little longer.

As he points into the distance to where we can just about make out the shapes of some of the buildings back in the city, I think about how far away it looks. I also think about how Mum is back there now, hopefully still in her bed, but possibly not.

'Why did you ask me about other girls?' Daryl suddenly says, proving that the awkward question I just posed a moment ago is still on his mind.

'I was just teasing you,' I reply, but Daryl doesn't smile or laugh.

He just goes very quiet and as he does, the bird above seems to tire of the pair of us and flies away, leaving us in complete silence now.

Why isn't Daryl talking anymore?

Why has he gone quiet?

And why did he seem to get weird just as soon as I mentioned other girls?

21

DAWN

The sun is up, and while we've only been on the road for ten minutes, I am already starting to see signs of the traffic that Los Angeles is notorious for. No sooner has a new day dawned than the inhabitants of this pretty but overcrowded city have started to leave their homes and clog up the highways, and that is making it a little more time-consuming for us to get to where we need to be. But the journey is made even more complicated thanks to what I saw just before we started it.

I know about that gun in the glove compartment, and I know now that Harvey has lied to me about owning a firearm.

The only question is - *why?*

I didn't ask Harvey as he got in behind the wheel and started the engine because, just like the photo in the basement, I'm afraid of what the answer might be, as well as afraid of potentially spooking someone who might have dangerous secrets to hide. But I didn't get much chance to say anything even if I'd wanted to because once we were on the road, Harvey had enlightened me about where he thought Daryl and Ellie might have gone.

'There's a place he goes to sometimes to watch the sunrise,' Harvey had said. 'It's a little way out of the city, but I know the route.'

Now we're on the road, I'm feeling a little bit better about things than I was back at the house and not just because we're on the move. It's because Ellie being taken to witness a pleasant sunrise is not the worst thing that could happen to her, and it's certainly far preferable than all the horror scenarios I was imagining in my head back in that basement earlier. But as the traffic in front of the windscreen builds and Harvey is forced to slow our progress a little by tapping the brakes more often than I'd like, my anxiety slowly but surely starts to gnaw away again little by little with every passing minute.

I know the main cause of that anxiety is the photo of Daryl with the missing woman from the posters, and suddenly, as we prepare to drive onto yet another freeway in this city that seems to be full of them, I spot her again.

Here is yet another poster showing Aubree's face, and it is taped to a lamppost by the side of this road, and as I stare at it, I get confirmation that it is her who I saw in the photo in the basement.

Daryl definitely knew her, and she definitely knew him.

That means Harvey must know her too, right?

'I'm sorry for being so paranoid,' I say as we enter the freeway and move at a good pace for the first time in a few minutes. 'I guess I've been a little nervous from seeing all those missing person posters around the city with that poor girl who looks to be around the same age as Ellie.'

I needed a way to broach the subject of Aubree's mysterious disappearance without making it obvious to Harvey that I had seen that photo in his basement, and I think I might have just done that.

'That's perfectly understandable,' Harvey says as he drives us on. 'You aren't the first parent in this city to be worried about their children, especially with what's happened recently.'

'I just don't understand how she could vanish and nobody know what happened to her,' I say. 'All these posters everywhere, and no one has seen her. How can that be? Somebody must know something, right?'

Maybe I'm pushing my luck a little bit, but I want to see how Harvey reacts when I press him on this topic. If he has nothing to hide, then he should have no problem discussing it with me. But if he does, or rather, if his son does, then he will most likely shell up and go quiet or defensive.

'This is a very big city in a very big country,' Harvey says, seemingly not skipping a beat. 'Maybe it's different in England, but it's much harder to find somebody who goes missing over here. There are over 300 million people in America, not to mention our close proximity to the Canadian and Mexican borders. Whether Aubree was kidnapped or if she just decided to disappear of her own accord, finding her is not going to be easy.'

That all makes sense, I suppose, but I still can't believe that somebody can just vanish without a trace. Can I also believe that Daryl and Harvey don't know what happened to her?

'But surely somebody must have some idea? Her family and friends?' I suggest, getting closer to the real point I'm making. 'I mean, all the people who knew her in this city. They have to have some clue. Or an opinion or theory, at least.'

'Maybe, but opinions and theories aren't facts,' Harvey says as he increases our speed, and I notice that we are leaving the city.

I'm just about to ask Harvey a few more leading questions surrounding Aubree and the people who might have known her but before I can, the driver speaks again.

'I understand your worry. You'd do anything for Ellie, and I get that. I'm the same with Daryl. I'd do anything for my son. Anything. All that matters to me is that he is safe. It's been that way since the day he was born, but I guess it's even more imperative now that his mother is no longer with us. It might sound selfish, but he's all I've got left, much like Ellie is for you. I'm just saying this because I don't want you to be embarrassed or feel like you overreacted when we find Daryl and Ellie safe and well in about half an hour's time. Okay?'

I hear everything Harvey has to say, but what I'm struck most by is the confidence with which he speaks of finding our children safe and well. He seems assured that there is no problem here, so maybe there isn't.

Or maybe he is just driving me out into this desert to hurt me like Daryl has already hurt Ellie.

They would never get away with this if they killed us, I tell myself silently as we drive on, although that is more of a wish than a hard fact I can fully lean on. *Everyone back home knows we came to see them. Unlike that missing woman on the poster, the police would know where to look if we went missing, and they would be looking right at Harvey and Daryl. So chill out, everything will be fine.*

'What do you think of the desert?' Harvey asks me as we move deeper into the remote, rain-deprived place. 'Not much out here, is there?'

I can't argue with that as I look at the mountains in the distance. There really isn't much of anything at all here.

But somewhere in amongst this inhospitable place is my daughter.

And that is why I won't stop searching until I find her.

22

ELLIE

'Come on, it's not far,' Daryl says to me as he tries to convince me to follow him along another trail on this mountain, the same mountain we just watched the spectacular sunrise from. 'It's about ten minutes down here, and I promise you'll love it when you get there.'

'No, I want to go back now,' I reply, repeating what I've already said to my boyfriend several times since we got back to our feet and stepped away from the cliff edge. I know the car is just on the other side of those boulders, and all I want to do is get back in it so we can drive to the city and I can see Mum again before she wakes up and finds me gone. But Daryl doesn't want to do that and prefers to not only stay out here, but keep going further into the wilderness, all in the name of showing me something else that I might like.

Perhaps if he hadn't got so weird and quiet when I mentioned other girls earlier, then I would be more willing to follow him to the next place. But I sensed a shift in him when I did, and that's why I feel awkward around him again, just like I did when we were in the car driving out here. I hate that I feel like I can't trust him fully yet, but it's only natural because I'm still getting to know him. Maybe if he didn't give me any reason to get worried, then it would be easier, but right now, all he is doing is making me more anxious.

'Come on, Ellie. What's the problem? You've come all this way to see me, so let me show you around,'

Daryl says, frustration creeping into his voice as he beckons for me to join him by the trail.

'I'm just really tired,' I try. 'I hardly slept. Maybe we could come back later in the week when I'm more in the mood for it.'

I hope that will work, and it sure is better than me being truthful. The fact is I feel on edge, not just because Daryl is being a little strange, but because we don't have deserts back home or large birds that circle overhead and make strange noises. I'm in unfamiliar territory, and I know I'd feel much better if we were somewhere more populated. Just being around a few other people would make me less worried, but now, even with Daryl, I feel a little isolated. And all Daryl wants to do is take me somewhere even quieter and more isolated than here.

'But it's such a long drive out here. We might not have time to come back again,' Daryl says. 'Come on, let's go.'

Daryl turns and heads along the trail then, but even though I don't want to go, I feel like I have no choice but to follow him because he has the car keys, so there's not much I can do without them. I couldn't even go and sit in the car, never mind drive out of here. All I would be left to do is stand out here by myself as the sun gets higher and hotter and the clock keeps ticking, increasing the chances of Mum waking up and finding me gone.

I have to go with him, don't I?

'What is this place?' I ask as I slowly start to follow.

'You'll see,' Daryl replies.

Another vague answer. But then I have an idea.

'I'll only come with you if you admit that I'm not the first girl you have brought here before,' I say and when I do, Daryl stops walking and pauses, his back still turned to me but his momentum temporarily halted. 'I don't mind you admitting it. I just want you to be honest with me.'

I wait to see what Daryl will say to that, but it takes a while for him to turn around and speak. When he does, he looks coy.

'Okay, you're not the first girl I've brought here,' he admits.

'See? That wasn't so hard, was it?' I say, shrugging. 'Why did you have to act all weird when I mentioned it?'

'I just wanted this place to feel special to you and didn't think it would do if you knew I'd brought someone else here.'

'It's still special,' I say, approaching Daryl. 'I'm here now, and she isn't.'

I take Daryl's hand when I reach him before giving him a kiss, one he accepts, but I still sense some awkwardness within him.

I decide to try and remove that by walking with him to show that I am willing to go to this next place now he has been honest with me, but as we go, I have one more question.

'So, what was her name?' I ask him, and Daryl stiffens again when I do.

'Her name?'

'Yeah. The last girl you brought here.'

'Why do you care?'

'I think it's healthy to talk about our exes. It's part of our past, right? I'm just trying to get to know you better, that's all. You can ask me anything about my ex-boyfriends too.'

That open invitation is supposed to make Daryl more relaxed during this conversation, but it doesn't seem to work.

'I'd rather just focus on this relationship rather than my old ones,' Daryl says, which is sweet, I suppose, but also a very sneaky way of avoiding the subject.

'Me too, but I think it's important. Come on, tell me, how many girls did you bring here?'

'Just one.'

I guess that answer is better than five or six.

'What was her name?' I ask again as we continue to walk slowly along the trail, getting further from the car.

'Erm.'

It's hardly a difficult question, but Daryl seems to be having a hard time remembering the name of his last girlfriend. I wait though, making it clear he has to answer me before we can carry on, and finally, he offers up a name.

'Rebecca.'

That didn't sound entirely convincing.

'Is that her real name, or have you just made one up because you don't want me to go looking for her on social media?' I jest, but Daryl doesn't laugh.

'No, that's her name.'

'Okay, now we're getting somewhere. See, this is fun,' I say, nudging Daryl playfully. 'So what happened with this *Rebecca*? How did she go from being somebody you brought here to being somebody you don't see anymore?'

The trail gets narrower at this point, and we have to walk single file, which is when Daryl invites me to walk ahead of him while he follows behind.

I do as he suggests, and as we pass between the narrowing walls of the boulders on either side of my shoulders, I think about how this is an adventure that could easily go wrong at any moment. I've seen enough films where people get stuck in remote places like this one to make me be careful about losing my footing and spraining an ankle or, worse, getting wedged in between a tight space and being unable to move.

'We just broke up,' Daryl replies, his voice quiet even though he is standing right behind me.

I pause then and turn back to him, but he just encourages me to carry on, so I do but so do my questions.

'Why did you break up?'

'We just did.'

'There must be a reason.'

'I guess we drifted apart.'

I laugh at that because it's not a common reason for young people to separate.

'You make it sound like you had been married for thirty years,' I say with a chuckle before the smile is wiped off my face when I accidentally brush the rough surface of a boulder with my right shoulder and feel it start to sting. 'Ouch.'

'You okay?'

'Yeah, I'm fine,' I say, but that did hurt a little, and I'm growing impatient of walking down this narrow trail. 'Are we nearly there?'

'Yeah, just a little further,' Daryl says before actually giving me a gentle push from behind as if to speed me up. But while he might have meant that in a playful way, it makes me feel very rushed, and I don't really appreciate it. But fortunately, he was right about it not being far because all of a sudden the trail widens out again, and I see now that we are in some kind of a clearing.

The clearing is surrounded on all sides by canyon walls, and with the sun still low in the sky, it's very shady and quite gloomy in here.

Is this it? Is this what Daryl has been so desperate to show me?

A barren clearing in the middle of some deserted canyon?

'What is this place?' I ask him as I look around at the red soil by my feet and the towering walls that ascend up towards the blue sky.

'This is what makes this place special,' Daryl says as he looks around too.

'I thought you brought me here to see the sunrise?' I ask, looking around and still feeling confused. 'What is there to see here?'

I guess I would have been about to get the answer to that question a second later as Daryl prepared to speak again. But he pauses when he hears the sound of a car engine nearby.

I hear it too, although it's weird because I didn't expect anybody else to come out here, considering how remote it is.

By the looks of it, neither did Daryl because now he looks very annoyed.

Dare I say it, he almost looks angry.

I guess that's because we've been interrupted.

But by whom?

And what exactly have we been interrupted from?

23

DAWN

We've found Daryl's car, but as yet, we haven't found Daryl or Ellie themselves.

Harvey parked up beside his son's vehicle two minutes ago, and the fact that he found it proved he was right in guessing where Daryl had gone, if it was a guess and not something else.

Something more sinister, like him leading me out here into danger too.

As I look around, I have a high vantage point from which to view the sprawling desert below us, as well as a better indication of just how far we are from the city, and I can't believe Ellie agreed to come all the way out here at such a ridiculous time of day. It's barely 6 am, but thanks to this being summer, at least the sun is up now, and it's already warm.

I swat away an annoying fly that buzzes around my face before asking Harvey where exactly our kids are supposed to be.

'Up here,' Harvey says, pointing the way, and I follow him up a path between two boulders to a place with an even better view of the desert. But it's not the view that I'm most interested in at the moment. Rather, it's the very steep cliff edge we are standing upon.

'This is dangerous,' I observe, not liking the idea of Ellie having been here.

'It's a great place to watch a sunrise,' Harvey muses, but we're already too late for that. It seems we're also too late to catch Ellie and Daryl.

'I can't see them,' I say, stating the obvious.

'No, but they're still around because the car is here,' Harvey says before he heads towards another trail. 'I'm guessing they have gone this way.'

'How did your son find this place?' I ask as I follow him, and it's the most obvious question because this is very far from the beaten track and not somewhere a person could easily expect to stumble across accidentally.

'I brought him here when he was younger,' Harvey tells me. 'Then Daryl came back here when he was trying to get away from everything with his mother, and this is about as far away from it all as one can get.'

'So, how did you find out he went here?'

'I followed him one day.'

Hearing Harvey's admission makes me feel slightly less guilty about getting so worked up about Ellie and always wanting to know where she is too.

I'm just about to ask Harvey if he's not troubled by the fact that Daryl has a penchant for disappearing into remote areas where nobody is supposed to know what he is doing, when we hear movement up ahead, and suddenly, we find the people we are looking for.

'Mum, what are you doing here?' Ellie cries when she sees me at the other end of the trail.

'Making sure you're okay,' I say as I quickly look her up and down to ascertain just that. But she looks fine, so I don't have to worry as much anymore. That is until I look at Daryl standing behind her and remember that photograph in the basement.

'I'm fine,' Ellie exclaims, clearly annoyed that I would stalk her out here, and Daryl is just as irritated with his father.

'I can't believe you followed us,' he says.

'We didn't follow you,' Harvey explains. 'I just guessed where you might have been. We both were worried when we woke up and found you had left without telling us where you were going.'

'We're not little kids,' Daryl says, and Ellie agrees with that sentiment, although she doesn't look quite as annoyed to have been interrupted as her boyfriend is. I get further proof of that fact when she walks towards me, clearly having lost interest in whatever was down the trail where she has just come from.

'Is everything okay?' I ask Ellie quietly when she's closer to me, and she just nods her head. 'How was the sunrise?' Harvey asks, but Daryl ignores that question, not that Harvey lets it knock him off his stride too much. 'It's a beautiful morning. What do you guys say we drive back to the city and find somewhere to get breakfast? I could go for some pancakes right about now.'

Food does sound appealing, as does getting out of here and going back to civilisation, so I agree with Harvey's idea and set off back to the cars. Ellie follows me, and while Harvey and Daryl bring up the rear, I get the chance to quietly ask Ellie another question.

'Are you sure everything's okay? With Daryl, I mean.'

'Yeah, why wouldn't it be?'

'You shouldn't have just left with him like that. You should have told me where you were going. What if something had happened and we hadn't been able to find you?'

'I'm fine.'

'Are you sure? You don't look it.'

Ellie realises then that I have registered there is something troubling her, and that feels like a good moment to tell her about what is troubling me, namely Daryl and his connection to the missing woman, a connection he has so far chosen to keep secret, as has his father. But before I can say anything, Harvey speaks up again.

'Dawn, you come with me again. Daryl and Ellie will meet us at the restaurant for breakfast. He knows where to go.'

Daryl nods his head to confirm he knows the next meeting place, but I'm not so keen on us splitting up again. But what else can we do? Neither Ellie nor I are insured to drive here, so Harvey and Daryl have to be behind the wheel.

Unless…

'I'll go with Ellie,' I say, suggesting I accompany her in the car with Daryl, though both Daryl and Harvey don't seem to be too impressed by that idea.

'Am I really such bad company?' Harvey asks me, feigning offence.

'No, of course not. I just-'

'Same seats. Don't worry, we'll all be back together again in no time,' Harvey says before reaching the car and opening the passenger door for me.

Daryl and Ellie get in their vehicle, so I reluctantly get in mine, and then we're all back on the road once again. But at least I can keep my eyes on my daughter now, or at least the car she is travelling in, and I do just that as we drive back through the desert towards the city, my glance never too far away from the rear-view mirror that allows me to see Daryl's car behind us.

'So, what do you think of your first trip into the desert?' Harvey asks me. 'There's not too much to see out here, is there?'

'No, not really,' I agree.

'Still, it's pretty cool, though, right? All this open space. I mean, it's not quite as green as your countryside, but it's good to get out in nature.'

'I suppose.'

Harvey makes the effort to keep the conversation flowing as we return to LA, but I don't say half as much as him until we are getting out of the car outside a small diner with a yellow neon sign hanging above it.

'Here we go. Best pancakes in town!' Harvey proudly declares as Daryl's car parks up nearby.

I wait for Ellie to join us before all four of us enter the diner, and after we have been seated at a booth in the back corner, I try to momentarily keep myself distracted with the menu as well as all the smells of the fried food and coffee that dominate this place.

I'm desperate to talk to Ellie in private and ask her if she knows that Daryl was close to Aubree, but I guess I'll have to wait until we get back to the house before I can do that. In the meantime, I need to fuel up, and after ordering blueberry pancakes upon Harvey's recommendation, I wait for my meal to arrive while Harvey and Daryl tell Ellie and me all about this diner and some of the famous people who have eaten here in the past. The proof of that is in the photos that hang on the wall around this cosy venue, showing the various chefs and waitresses with all manner of A-List celebrities from years gone by, but while Ellie studies a few of those, I look out of the window at the busy car park and when I do, I spot something.

It's yet another poster of that missing woman.

Everyone in this city wants to know what happened to her, including me.

But what if the only people who know are the ones sitting opposite me at this table?

24

ELLIE

It was definitely a strange start to the day, from Daryl taking me out to see the sunrise in the desert to Mum showing up unexpectedly with Harvey. But things settled down a little after we went back to the city and had breakfast, and after that, things went more as I had expected them to when I flew out here.

Harvey and Daryl showed me and Mum several sights around LA, and we had a blast.

We went into Beverly Hills and had a walk along Rodeo Drive, one of the most expensive streets in the world thanks to all the designer stores that are located there. I took Mum inside several glamorous shops, although we didn't buy much, not because we didn't see anything we liked, but because we didn't see anything we could afford. After that, we drove to the coast, and while the traffic was a nightmare getting there, it was worth it when we got to Santa Monica and had a walk along the pier, passing the fitness freaks working out on Muscle Beach and taking photos of the sea and the famous Pacific Wheel. We then had lunch in a lovely outdoor café nearby before walking to Venice Beach and seeing the canals, as well as stopping off along the way to watch all the people with their shirts off playing basketball or skateboarding along the front.

I loved it there and wanted to stay longer, but Mum was getting a little sunburnt, and Harvey suggested we get back before rush hour, so we returned to the cars and drove home, and now, after what feels like the longest day ever after getting up so early, I'm back at the house and ready to relax.

And by relax, I mean get in the swimming pool with a cup of wine.

My plan is to get changed quickly in my bedroom before going back down to join Harvey and Daryl, who are already in the back garden and enjoying the last few hours of sun, but before I can do that, Mum enters the bedroom and closes the door behind her.

'I need to talk to you about something,' she says as I am busy deciding whether to wear my blue bikini or my red one.

'What's up?' I ask as I decide on red.

'I saw something in the basement this morning,' Mum says as she approaches me.

'Basement?'

'Yep, they have a basement. They didn't show us when we got here, but I found it.'

'What's down there?'

'Mainly a lot of boxes full of Harvey's wife's things.'

'What were you doing snooping around?'

'I wasn't snooping around. Okay, maybe a little bit. But it's a good job I was because I found something.'

'What?'

'I found a photo of Daryl and another woman,' Mum tells me, but I'm not sure if that is supposed to be shocking to me. If so, it's not because I already know that I'm not Daryl's first girlfriend, nor could I have expected to be, considering he's in his mid-twenties.

'So what?' I say, annoyed because I want to undress and change into this bikini, but Mum is still lingering around.
'The woman he was with is the same woman who is on all those missing person posters around the city. It's Aubree.'
'What?'
Credit to Mum. She has managed to get my attention, and now I care less about the bikini and more about what she is saying.
'Daryl was with that missing woman. He knows her, or at least he knew her before whatever happened to her.'
I think about that for a moment, but I'm not sure what I'm supposed to do with this information.
'Okay, so she was a friend or something. So what?'
'I think she was more than a friend,' she says before showing me the photo on her phone. When I look, I see Daryl with his arm around a woman, and it looks like the image was captured here at this house, out by the pool, so I'm guessing it was Harvey who took it.
'Okay, so she might have been his girlfriend,' I say with a shrug. 'And?'
'So you didn't know about this?'
'No.'
'Don't you think it's weird that he hasn't told you that he knew her? Neither has Harvey. Both of them have kept quiet about it even when I asked them about the missing woman in the car yesterday.'
'And?'
'What are they hiding?'
'Nothing.'

'Really? Then why not tell us that they knew her? There must be a reason they don't want to say. There must be a reason they are keeping it a secret from us.'

I can see that Mum has clearly put a lot of thought into this and has no doubt come up with all sorts of conspiracy theories, but I'm not getting quite as worked up as she is about it all yet because I'm sure there is a perfectly reasonable explanation for why they didn't tell us.

But what could it be? I have asked Daryl a couple of times now about his ex-partners, including as recently as this morning when we were out in the desert, but he didn't mention that missing woman. All he did was get awkward.

Is this why?

Was he nervous because he didn't want to talk about her?

Is Rebecca real, or was that somebody else? Maybe it was a made-up name and he was covering up for something. Maybe he is hiding something, like Mum says. Maybe he took Aubree there.

Okay, congratulations, Mum.

Now I am curious too.

'Let's go and ask him,' I suggest, figuring that will be a simple way of finding out more about this. 'We can ask Harvey too.'

'No, we can't do that!' Mum cries, confusing me now.

'Why not?'

'Because it might be dangerous.'

'How is it dangerous?'

'What if they are the ones who hurt her?'

'What?'

I laugh at that suggestion because while I am eager to learn more about if Daryl and Harvey did know Aubree, it's definitely not because I think they might be the ones behind her disappearance. But Mum seems to think they might be, which is just crazy.

Isn't it?

'What if Daryl had something to do with her going missing?' Mum asks. 'Or Harvey? That would explain why they aren't telling anybody that they knew her, right?'

'Don't be stupid.'

'Think about it. If they didn't have anything to hide, then why not just say they knew her? If we knew somebody who went missing, then we would mention it, wouldn't we? Unless we were the reason that person had gone missing, in which case we'd keep quiet and not say a word, just like they have done!'

Mum seems to think that she has just cracked some case that the best minds in the LAPD haven't been able to crack themselves, but I still think this is all absurd.

'I'm going to ask Daryl now,' I say as I decide to ditch the bikini for the time being and just go back downstairs in my casual clothes. But before I can go, Mum grabs my arm and stops me.

'Ellie. Listen to me. We might not be safe here. We just need to make up an excuse and leave.'

'What? No way, we've only just got here!'

'But now we know something isn't right.'

'No, we don't. You just saw some photograph and have made up a crazy story in your head. It might not even be

Aubree. It might just be somebody who looks like her and that's why they haven't told us that they knew her.'

I try to pull away from Mum then, but she doesn't let me go.

'Ellie. Please. It's the same woman as in the poster. The photo was also in a box hidden away in a basement, a basement that neither of us were supposed to know about. I don't want Harvey or Daryl to know that I saw that photograph, which is why we can't just ask them. I also don't want them to panic if we are onto something because then they might hurt us. We just need to act normal but make up a reason to leave.'

'I'm not leaving!'

I finally manage to pull away from Mum's grasp and go for the door, but she hurries after me, and despite opening the door, Mum pushes it closed again quickly.

'Ellie. Please. We have to be careful.'

'Mum, you're overreacting!'

'Am I? I found a gun in Harvey's car! What about that?'

I was not expecting that.

'What?'

'It was in the glove compartment.'

'Okay, so what? This is America; everyone's got a gun.'

'He told us he didn't have one, remember? We explicitly asked him at dinner, and he said no. So he lied to us.'

I do remember that conversation, so it does seem that Harvey lied, but maybe it's not such a big deal.

'He probably just didn't want to scare us,' I suggest. 'Guns are weird to us, but they're normal here, and if he's got one, it means he's just being sensible and taking precautions to protect his property or whatever.'

But Mum doesn't like that answer.
'He lied to us. That's not very trustworthy. Now think about it. How much do we actually know about Daryl and Harvey? Only what they have told us about themselves. But they're hiding things, and now we're here in their house, we have to be cautious because what else might they be hiding?'
'Relax. Harvey is cool. And Daryl is not a problem. He's lovely.'
'Is he? He took you out into the middle of the desert without telling anybody.'
'It was romantic.'
'Maybe he did the same thing with Aubree, and maybe she thought it was romantic too. Right up until the moment he killed her and buried her in the dirt!'
'Mum!'
I can't believe Mum thinks Daryl killed Aubree, but she has more to say to me.
'What if we hadn't got there and interrupted you this morning?' she asks. 'What were you doing after the sunrise? Why had you gone further down the trail? What was Daryl supposed to be showing you there?'
'He took me to a clearing.'
'A clearing? Why?'
'He said something about it being special.'
'What was so special about it?'
'I don't know. We heard the car then, and you interrupted us.'
'How was Daryl behaving? Normally or was he being weird?'

'He was normal,' I say, but that's not strictly true, and Mum picks up on it.
'What is it?' she asks me, her hand still holding the bedroom door closed.
'He was getting a little awkward, I suppose,' I admit. 'I'd been asking him if he'd ever taken another girl there before.'
'Had he?'
'Yeah.'
Mum looks very troubled now as if she has all the confirmation that she needs that Daryl killed Aubree and buried her out there, and he was planning to do the exact same thing to me if she hadn't been able to intervene.
But that's just insane and not true.
Isn't it?

25

DAWN

It's been a couple of hours since I confronted Ellie in the bedroom upstairs and told her about Daryl's connection to the missing woman. So why are we still here and not somewhere else, a safe distance away where we can try and assess the situation and figure out if Daryl really is dangerous or not?

It's because Ellie begged me to stay quiet for a little while longer so she could have time to try and find out what Daryl's exact relationship with Aubree was.

I did not like the idea and reaffirmed my belief that we should have made up an excuse and gone somewhere else, but Ellie told me that she would not go with me, so what choice did I have? I'm not leaving her here, not until I know for sure that it's safe, so if she is staying, then so am I.

That is why I am currently sitting by the pool with Harvey as the sun sets, the dinner he just cooked for us still digesting in my stomach and a cup of red wine sitting on the table beside me. But I've barely touched my drink, although the same can't be said of the man who poured it for me. Harvey is already on his third measure, and if I didn't know any better, I would say that alcohol has clearly become a crutch for him since his wife passed.

While he was sober this morning and afternoon while he was driving us around, he hasn't hesitated to hit the bottle as the day draws to a close, and now he's no longer required to do anything other than sit around and reminisce. And reminisce is exactly what he is doing as he tells me yet another story about his life before his loss, while Ellie and Daryl sit on the sofa inside, watching a movie.

'I used to do so much travelling,' Harvey says as I glance at the double doors and make sure I can still see my daughter on the other side of the glass sitting beside her boyfriend because the last thing I need is those two sneaking off again.

'But travelling was always easier with a companion by my side,' Harvey goes on. 'Jodie and I had so many places we hadn't ticked off our bucket list yet. Australia. Peru. Portugal. I know I could go there now, but it just wouldn't be the same, not without her. What about you?'

Harvey turns to me and my untouched wine.

'Me?'

'Yeah. You must have had places you wanted to go to with Sean. Do you think you'd still go there, or would it be too hard?'

'Oh, I don't know. That's not the only issue. It's the money side of things too.'

'Yeah, that's a good point,' Harvey says. 'It's much tougher to plan exciting trips on one income instead of two.'

Harvey reaches for the bottle again and is clearly enjoying this pity party. Or maybe he is just not used to having adult company and can't talk about things like this with his son. Either way, I'm not sure it's the healthiest thing for the pair of us to be talking about the past and how our lives are not quite as good as they once were.

But then Harvey surprises me by talking about the future.

'I do want to meet somebody else,' he confesses. 'Being in a relationship is a wonderful thing, and I know I want to experience it again, though it does feel weird to think about being intimate with another woman.'

Harvey sighs as he refills his cup before noting that my drink does not seem to be going down.

'Can I get you anything else? I have some spirits inside if you'd prefer something other than wine?'

'No, I'm fine, thank you,' I say. 'I'm just tired. It was a very early start.'

'It sure was.'

Harvey puts the bottle back down then, or at least what's left of the bottle, because he's almost drained the whole thing by himself. But despite the brief interlude, he resumes his train of thought right where he left off a moment ago, returning to the rather awkward subject of whether or not he could move on with a new woman.

As he ponders the idea out loud, no doubt fuelled by all the drinks he has consumed over the last hour, I think about how we had a similar conversation last night, and it was one that left me feeling a little uneasy. That was because I was concerned the two of us might have had 'a moment' at one point, and that would be entirely inappropriate considering our children are currently dating.

I'm so afraid of something like that happening again that I don't say much to Harvey as he talks, giving him very little to go off in terms of what I might be thinking. That might be a good thing because my thoughts are mainly dominated by one thing, and that is whether or not his son is trouble.

I am thinking about what Ellie told me she was going to do and, more specifically, if it will lead to anything. She is going to try and figure out how close Daryl was to Aubree using various means available to someone like her, and that means a lot of social media stalking and internet searching. But I guess that is okay as long as it's all she does. I told her up in that bedroom earlier that under no circumstances is she to directly come out and tell Daryl that she knows he was with Aubree in the past. That might spook Daryl if he has anything to hide, and seeing as that photo is stuffed away in a box in the basement, I suspect he might have.

If I had my way, I would be sitting in a police station somewhere in downtown Los Angeles right about now, enlightening an officer there about Daryl and how he seems to want to keep quiet about the fact that he knew a missing woman. If the police were not aware of his connection to her, then they would surely be interested in coming over to this house and asking him a few questions, and why shouldn't they? It's only a problem if he has something to hide. But if he does, maybe this city and, most importantly, that poor woman's family, will finally get some answers as to what happened.

Alas, Ellie has told me to be patient, and at the risk of pushing her away and further into potential danger, I have had to respect her wishes in order to stay close enough to her to make sure she is safe. Maybe I am just running on a severe lack of sleep and am all discombobulated by being halfway across the globe, and that could be why I have this crazy idea that Daryl might have something to do with Aubree going missing.

I genuinely hope that is all it is, just me being silly.

But just in case it's not, I will keep a very close eye on Ellie.

She is under strict instructions not to go off with Daryl by herself again.

But as the sky gets darker and all of our bedtimes draw nearer, I wonder if she will obey the wishes of her paranoid mother or if she will do something foolish once again.

26

ELLIE

Daryl and I spent the last two hours watching a movie, but all I really wanted to be doing in that time was be looking online to figure out the connection between my boyfriend and Aubree.

I did have a go at starting to snoop while on the sofa beside Daryl, but he noticed me on my phone straight away and assumed I wasn't enjoying the film he'd chosen for us to watch. I told him that wasn't the case, but to prove it, I put my phone down and focused on the TV screen from then on.

One of the things I liked about Daryl when we first got talking was that he told me he was making an effort to spend less time on his phone, and I had told him I was trying to do the same, so it would have been out of character for me to be on my device so much in front of him. It also carried the risk of him seeing what I was doing, or rather, who I was searching for on social media, so I have left it until a better time.

Now, that better time is here.

All four of us in the house went to bed around half an hour ago, and now we are all in our rooms with the lights turned off, I have more privacy to look at Aubree's online presence. Daryl is beside me, but he's already asleep, worn out by the fact that we got out of bed at a silly time this morning. But while I am just as exhausted as he is and can barely stop myself from yawning every thirty seconds, I plan on staying awake a little longer until I have had a proper look on all of Daryl's social media accounts as well as the accounts that used to belong to the missing woman and find any potential links.

Of course, there have been no recent updates on any of Aubree's accounts, making it even more likely that she has come to harm because if she was safe and well somewhere, then she would most likely have updated her followers online as to where she was and what she was doing. But all is quiet on her social media pages as it has been on Daryl's recently, proving that he has been trying to be true to his word and use his phone less. But while both have been quiet in recent times, the great thing about the internet is that they show plenty of historical things too. Dad used to say to me before he died that I was to be careful with what I put online because I was leaving fingerprints all over the internet that would never be deleted, but I just used to laugh at that and tell him not to be so dramatic. But now I'm a little older, I realise how right he was, just like I realise how right he was about so many other things that I took no heed of at the time.

Finding the part of Facebook that lists all of Daryl's 'Friends', I type in Aubree's name to see what comes up, though I get no results. But just to be thorough, I proceed to Aubree's Facebook account and do the same thing there, only this time, I am searching for Daryl's name amongst the list of her friends.

And then I get a hit.

Aubree has Daryl listed amongst her friends on Facebook, proving Mum was right and adding more credibility to that photo she showed me. They did know each other. But if she was 'friends' with him, why does she not appear in his list of friends. It's common practice for people to add each other, isn't it?

Unless they did at one point but Daryl has since deleted her from his account.

I wonder if he could have done that. If so, that would be a little troubling, but for the time being, I still have plenty of work to do. Now that I have established a connection between the pair, I need to see if there is anything more. And so begins my painstaking search through all the photo albums belonging to Aubree to see if Daryl appears in any of the images she has uploaded over the years.

Opening various albums, ones that have titles like 'Spring Break Baby!' and 'I Love LA', I keep clicking as photo after photo flashes up on my screen. But while I see plenty of pictures of Aubree with different guys, most of them presumably friends from high school and college, I fail to find any sign of Daryl on here and certainly nothing that suggests he might have been her boyfriend at one point.

The only pictures I find that even hint at some of Aubree's previous relationships are the ones in the photo album titled 'West Coast Road Trip!' and there are several images in there of Aubree with a guy with short dark hair. He has been tagged in the photos, so I can see that his name is Cody Jones, and he certainly looked to be close to Aubree, even kissing her in one photo, which was uploaded just over a year ago. I wonder what happened to this Cody guy, so I click his name to go onto his profile page and once there, I have a quick look down at some of his most recent posts.

At first, it seems there is nothing more significant here than a few images of him surfing, but then I start to find a few references to Aubree in which he mentions her by name and says how he wishes she would be found safe and well. Another post says how she was a great girl, and he can't believe she has gone missing. And there is even a status update from him saying that he was spoken to by the police due to him being an ex-boyfriend, but nothing came of it because he has nothing to hide and would always care about Aubree even though they were no longer together.

I guess he had nothing to do with it if the police didn't deem him worthy of more questioning, so I leave his profile and return to Aubree's but just as I do that, Daryl stirs in the bed, and despite trying my best to pretend to be asleep too, he catches me looking at my phone before I can put it down.

'What's up? Don't tell me you can't sleep again,' he says as he puts his arm around me and snuggles into my back.

'Yeah, it's weird. My body clock is all over the place,' I tell him, but that admission only seems to make Daryl think that I might need something else to tire me out, and he starts to kiss my neck.

While that would normally be something I would be highly receptive to, I don't quite enjoy it as much with this load on my mind, and when Daryl gets that impression, he stops kissing me and asks me again if

I'm alright. That's when I go against the advice Mum gave me and do the thing I promised her I wouldn't do.

'Do you know Aubree?' I ask Daryl as I roll over to try and get a better look at him.

'What?'

'The missing woman on all those posters. Do you know her?' I repeat.

'No,' Daryl replies firmly.

'Then why has she got you as a friend on Facebook?'

It might be dark in this bedroom with all the lights off but even through the gloom, I distinctly make out the sight of Daryl's eyebrows rising up as if he is surprised that I have just said such a thing.

'What?'

'You're Facebook friends,' I repeat. 'So you two must know each other, right?'

Daryl doesn't say anything for a moment, a fact that does little to make me believe what he says when he eventually offers up an explanation.

'We went to the same high school,' he tells me. 'So I guess we knew each other. But I wouldn't call us friends. I don't think I ever spoke to her in my life.'

'You never spoke?'

'No, we just went to the same school years ago. That'll be why she added me. You know how it is. People add each other on social media all the time based on having attended the same school together. I don't recognise half the people I have as friends on Facebook because I've forgotten half of them and haven't spoken to many of them in years. Aubree was just some girl who attended the same school as me, but she was one of hundreds.'

'So why did you say you didn't know her when I asked you?'

'Because I didn't know her. I just told you we went to school together, but we never spoke. She doesn't appear on my Facebook account as a friend because I don't class her as someone I knew.'

'Knew? Why the past tense?'

'What?'

'Why did you say knew instead of know? As if she's no longer alive.'

'What are you talking about?'

'You talked about her in the past tense.'

'So what?'

'So, she's still missing. She might be alive.'

'No, she isn't.'

'What?'

I freeze when I hear Daryl say such a cold thing so easily as if he knows it to be fact. But it's not a fact because nobody else in this city seems to know what happened to her.

So how can Daryl be so sure?

'How do you know she's dead?' I ask him when he hasn't spoken again.

'Well, I don't know for a fact, but surely it's obvious by now that something bad happened to her,' he says. 'She hasn't made contact with her family or friends in three months, so she must be dead, right?'

Daryl seems to just have been making an assumption rather than speaking from a place of actual knowledge, which I suppose is a big relief. But I still don't like how he lied to me about not knowing Aubree because even if they weren't strictly friends in the truest sense of the word, he could have mentioned that he went to the same school as her without me pushing him on it, couldn't he?

'So you weren't close?' I ask him as my final question before dropping the subject, and after Daryl has once again wholeheartedly denied knowing Aubree very well at all, I leave it and roll over on my pillow.

Daryl gives me a kiss before telling me to get some sleep, before he rolls over to do the same thing.

But I am not going to go to sleep.

I'm going to wait until he has drifted off.

Then I am going to try and get the hell out of here.

That's because he is lying to me, and the photo on Mum's phone proves it.

27

DAWN

Sleep should be coming easily to me on account of how little of it I've actually had over the last couple of days, but it's the furthest thing from my mind as I lie in bed and wonder what is going on with Ellie and Daryl.
She said she was going to do some research into Aubree online, so I wonder how that is going. But that's not the main reason why I'm keeping myself awake. That would be because I am making sure that the pair of star-crossed lovers do not try and sneak out of the house again and disappear into the desert, and the best way to do that is to listen out for any movement in the hallway.

It's about one o'clock in the morning when I hear footsteps outside my bedroom door, and I'm just about to jump out of bed and go and catch whoever it is creeping around when my door opens, and I see Ellie walk in. It's dark, but I'd recognise her body shape and gait anywhere, and once she has closed the door, I turn on the bedside lamp and ask her what is wrong. But before she answers that, she has a surprising statement for me.

'Okay,' Ellie says with a deep sigh. 'We need to leave.'

'What?'

While I'm happy because leaving was the plan I suggested yesterday, I'm unsure how Ellie has suddenly changed her mind on the matter because she was in total disagreement with me before we went to bed.

'What happened?' I ask, fearful for the answer because I'm hoping it doesn't involve Daryl threatening her if he figured out that we are suspicious of him now.

'I had a look at Aubree's Facebook profile and saw that she had Daryl as a friend,' Ellie explains. 'Then I asked him if he knew her.'

'You weren't supposed to mention her by name,' I remind her, but Ellie dismisses my concerns and urges me to keep my voice down because Daryl and Harvey are still asleep.

'After you showed me the photo, I had to ask him outright if he knew her,' Ellie tells me. 'I had to see if he would tell the truth or lie.'

'And?'

'He lied. He admitted they went to the same school together but said that was it. He doesn't have her as a friend on his Facebook account, and he said he barely knew her. But he was uncomfortable talking about it, and I could tell there was more. They looked so close in that photo, so he is definitely lying about never having spoken to her, and it was a recent one, so it was not taken at school years ago. They knew each other recently, but he's not telling me that. That's why I want to go.'

Ellie looks impossibly sad, as she might well do, knowing that she is being lied to by somebody she loves and thought she could trust. But as heart-breaking as that must be for her, she's better to be safe than sorry, and now she wants to leave, we need to make a plan.

'I've been thinking about it, and we could tell them that we've had an unexpected death in the family,'

I suggest as Ellie stands by the side of my bed, looking sad. 'That would give us the excuse to have to leave early and fly back to England. What do you think?'

'They'll want to know who it is and what happened.'

'I suppose so, so let's figure it out. Let's say it was your great aunt Maggie, and she used to babysit you all the time. You adored her, and now she is gone, you don't want to miss the funeral, so you want to go back to be with family now, as do I. Okay?'

Ellie thinks about my story of a fictitious aunt Maggie for a moment before agreeing it just might work. But she does raise rather a good point a moment later.

'You'll have to help me. I'm a terrible liar,' she says, and I agree with her on that.

'Okay, let's pack my things up, then we'll go and deal with yours,' I reply, and together, the two of us start to refill my suitcase, working as quietly as we can as the aim is to have most of the packing done before we tell our hosts that we are leaving. That way, there should be less chance of them convincing us to stay.

Once my suitcase is full and I think I've got everything, I suggest Ellie goes to do the same thing, but this will be trickier because Daryl is sleeping in her room, and doing all the packing without waking him up will be nigh on impossible. It would also be very suspicious if she was to do such a thing without telling her boyfriend that she had to go, so that's why I suggest this is the part where she wakes Daryl and tells him what is going on.

'I'll come with you,' I say, knowing she'll most likely need me for backup should Daryl have lots of questions for her.

Following Ellie to her room, my mind is already on the tricky problem of having to book ourselves onto an earlier flight home than scheduled, but I guess I'll just have to deal with that when we get to the airport. For now, the important thing is to get out of this house because both Daryl and Harvey have been caught lying to us about two very troubling things: *Aubree and the gun.*

As I start gathering up Ellie's things that are strewn across the bedroom floor, Ellie gently shakes Daryl and when he wakes up, he sees her, me and the bedroom light on and quite rightly wonders what is going on.

Ellie begins running through her fabricated story, telling Daryl all about the fictional Maggie and how her death has come as such a shock. Before Daryl can say anything, I jump in and point out how she was a huge part of our family, and now we are needed back home at this difficult time so we can help with all the funeral arrangements, a necessary task that will be unpleasant but needs to be done quickly.

Daryl can clearly see that this is happening whether he wants it to or not because I continue packing as I talk, and once Ellie starts to help me, we get it done quickly, and soon enough, her suitcase is ready to join mine out in the hallway.

Now we just need to go and tell Harvey.

'Go and get our things from the bathroom,' I instruct Ellie before I go in search of the man of the house, and after knocking on his bedroom door and getting no answer, I enter his room and find him snoring away on his back.

I guess all that wine has knocked him out, but he's about to get a rude awakening now, and after he has failed to respond when I've called his name a couple of times, I give him a shake until he stirs from his deep sleep. Then I give him the exact same story we gave to Daryl, before adding that we are going to get a taxi to the airport now, and we hate to have to leave so abruptly like this, but it's just one of those things, unfortunately.

'I understand,' Harvey says, thankfully not disputing anything I've said, but rather than stay in bed, he goes to get up and then he tells me why. 'But don't worry about calling a cab. I'll drive you to the airport myself.'

'No, it's fine, I'll get a taxi. It's the middle of the night. You should sleep.'

'You're right, I should, but somehow, I don't think my son is going to be too pleased with Ellie leaving early, so if I don't offer to take you, then he will, and I'd much rather it be me driving through the city at this time of night than him.'

Harvey seems set on being the one to take us to the airport, and while it would have been much more comfortable for Ellie and I to take a taxi, I can't protest too much without making him wonder why we are so desperate to get away, so I am reluctantly forced to accept the offer.

Finding Ellie out in the hallway again, I tell her the new plan, before the men help carry our suitcases downstairs. It's clear to see that Daryl is upset for Ellie to be leaving so soon, and he tries a couple of times to have a quiet word with her, but I nip that in the bud as quickly as I can and make sure that Ellie doesn't get side-tracked and change her mind about going. But she doesn't do that, and once we walk out the front door and load our luggage into the back of Harvey's car, I guess we really are getting out of here.

As Ellie and Daryl take their places on the back seat and I sit in the front beside the driver, Harvey starts the engine.

Next stop LAX Airport.

Or at least I hope it is.

Unless Harvey and Daryl have figured out that we have an ulterior motive for wanting to leave so suddenly.

Then I guess they could drive us anywhere.

Like out into the desert again, and this time, we might not be coming back.

28

ELLIE

I know Mum would have had some concerns about Harvey driving us somewhere other than the airport if he figured out we were lying to him and Daryl about our reasons for leaving, but I wasn't so worried.

I knew Harvey would take us to LAX because we'd done a good job of selling them the story about my great aunt Maggie. But I suppose there was always a chance Harvey could have gone a different way, though once the signs for LAX became more frequent, I knew he was taking us where we had asked. That became more obvious when dozens of planes came into view as we passed one of the airport's perimeter fences, and by the time we parked beneath the large sign that said 'Departures', I knew we were really leaving. But Daryl knew it too, and that was why he had insisted on holding my hand all the way to the airport and by the time he let go, I swear he had a few tears in his eyes.

That was the moment I regretted what we were doing and considered stopping this charade.

But then I remembered the photo and how he had confidently lied to me, and even if there is an innocent reason for him doing that, I can't trust him at this moment in time, nor am I sure I can trust him again. If he can lie to me once, what would be stopping him lying again? It's crazy, but in just forty-eight hours, I've gone from thinking I'd found the man of my dreams and planning out a future life in America to wondering if this whole thing has just been one stupid waste of time.

What if Daryl has been seeing other girls while I've been in England?

What if lying comes so easily to him that he just can't help himself?

And what if moving here to be with him would have been the biggest mistake of my life?

I will have plenty of time to think about the answer to all those questions because there is an eleven-hour flight ahead of me, and as Mum and I say our goodbyes to our American hosts, I can't quite believe we're going back to England already.

'I'll come and see you next time,' Daryl tells me. 'Just let me know when you're ready for a visitor.'

I nod my head, though I'm totally unsure if I'll even message him when I get back home, never mind arrange for him to come and see me over there. Then Daryl wraps his arms around me and tells me he loves me before giving me a kiss, and my heart breaks a little more because if only everything was still perfect like I thought it was, then I could still be happy and excited for the future instead of being miserable and facing a return to my boring old life.

Meanwhile, Harvey is saying his own goodbye to Mum, giving her a hug too, although there is no kiss with this one, though he does seem almost as sad as Daryl to see us go. But Mum keeps her focus and thanks Harvey for allowing us to stay at his house, before going through the motions of saying he will be welcome at her place in the future.

With the goodbyes done, it's time for us to go inside the airport, so we give Daryl and Harvey one more wave before walking through the sliding doors and entering the air-conditioned terminal with all the different screens showing all the different flights and airline carriers.
I force myself to look back at Daryl and give him another wave, just to make it look like I really am torn about leaving him, but once we're out of view and standing in the line for one of the check-in desks, I can drop the act and when I do, I feel an overwhelming wave of sadness wash over me.
It takes Mum a little while to notice that I am crying because she is busy locating our passports in her handbag, but when she spots my tears, she stops what she is doing and puts her arms around me.
'Oh, love. I'm sorry,' she says when she sees that my heart is breaking, and despite being in a very public place, I bury my head in her chest and sob for several minutes, crying over the complete mess this trip has turned into.
I have no idea how I'll tell my friends what happened over here, as the last they heard, when I messaged them earlier, I was having the time of my life in LA. But things have changed fast, and now I'm coming home, feeling as single as I have ever been.
Mum approaches the check-in desk once I've calmed down and then begins to politely ask if there is a much earlier flight back to London that we can get on than the one we originally booked. The woman in the uniform doing the checking-in frowns before spending an awfully long time typing things into her computer before

announcing that she can put us on the 6 am out of here, but it's going to cost us an extra two thousand dollars.

I wince almost as much as Mum does, but before I can tell her that it's too much money and that we should do something else, Mum produces her credit card, the one she's only ever used in emergencies, and tells the woman to charge the flight to that. Despite my protests, Mum tells me to be quiet, and a few minutes later, we are given our printed boarding passes and watching our suitcases disappear down a conveyor belt into the bowels of the airport.

Security is a breeze because there's hardly anybody around at this hour, and while we are very early for our flight, we find a café that is open and get something to eat ahead of our long journey. I'm mostly quiet in the café, thinking about Daryl and LA and how I thought I had life figured out until I suddenly didn't. But Mum is quiet too until I ask her what she is doing on her phone, though when I do, I immediately wish I hadn't.

'I'm looking up the contact details for the LAPD,' she tells me casually as if that's a very normal thing to say over an airport breakfast.

'What?'

'The police, Ellie. I'm looking for their contact details.'

'Why?'

'Why do you think?' So I can get them to look into Daryl and see if he had anything to do with Aubree going missing.'

'You can't do that!'

'Why not?'

'Because he might be innocent!'

'And he might not be. But there's only one way to find out.'

Mum goes back to looking at her phone, or at least she does until I swipe it out of her hand. 'Hey, what are you doing?' Mum cries, and she tries to get her phone back, but I keep it out of reach for the time being.

'Just leave it,' I say. 'We've left them now, and my relationship is ruined. Aren't you happy enough?'

'Happy? Of course, I'm not happy. What are you talking about?'

'It's over; you won. You've got me back. I won't be moving to America to be with Daryl. I'll just be stuck at home with you forever. Isn't that what you want? You'll never have to be on your own if I'm around. We can just be two sad losers together.'

'Ellie!'

'No, just leave it!' I say, and I get up from my seat, leaving most of my breakfast untouched, but I was barely hungry anyway. No one with a broken heart ever has much of an appetite, and I'm no different.

'Ellie, come back!' Mum calls after me, attracting the attention of the few other early-bird passengers who are filtering into this café around us. But I ignore her, taking my carry-on bag and her phone with me, so she is forced to follow me and leave her breakfast behind too.

By the time she catches up with me, I'm already halfway to our gate, and even though there are still over two hours to our flight, I am willing to sit by the doors and say nothing else until we can board. But I'm forced to give Mum her phone back in the end, simply because she won't stop pestering me for it, though I keep a close eye on her to make sure she doesn't make any phone calls to the police.

Doesn't she see that to do such a thing would be a nightmare for us? The police would also want to question us if we gave them a tip off, and that might mean having to come back. Even if it didn't, it would mean Daryl and Harvey would know exactly why we left so suddenly, and I don't want them to know. Whatever has happened with Daryl and Aubree and caused him to lie to me is no longer any of my business, and I'm trying to make Mum see that it is none of hers too. It only concerned us when we were in their house, but now we're not, and we'll never see either Daryl or Harvey ever again.

Mum eventually agrees that she will leave it, and by the time the seats around the gate have filled up and the sun has risen over LAX, I know it's almost time to fly home, returning back to my life before I met Daryl.

Why did he have to lie to me?

Things could have been so great if he hadn't.

That's why it's impossible not to feel like I've lost something special as I hand my boarding pass over to the airline employee at the gate before making my way onto the plane. But just as I'm strapping myself into my very expensively purchased seat beside Mum, I have another feeling too, and it's a very strange one because I can't know for sure if it's justified, yet I still feel it, nevertheless.

I have the feeling I might have just had a very lucky escape.

29

DAWN

Returning to work after a holiday is always a tough time, and I can hardly say I'm feeling good as I go about my duties at the supermarket on yet another long and lonely night shift. But I'm not just feeling blue because I've gone from the sun-kissed streets of Los Angeles to the damp and dreary streets of my hometown again in such a short space of time. There are many other reasons for my downbeat demeanour, and I have plenty of time to ponder those reasons as I toil away through the night.

One of the biggest causes of my unhappiness is the fact that I spent two thousand dollars that I don't have on booking an early flight out of LA. Putting the cost of the impromptu tickets on my credit card might have bought me both the tickets and some time, but that time will run out soon when I have to start making the first payments back to the bank. In hindsight, I could have considered staying in California with Ellie until our flight was due to depart, but even if we had got a room in a hotel until then, we still would have ended up spending extra money that I didn't plan to spend when I first agreed to go over there and stay with Harvey and Daryl. The whole trip has ended up being a financial nightmare, and while I have returned to work early, it's going to take me many months of extra shifts to offset the cost of mine and my daughter's brief dalliance with the United States.

But even with money worries on my mind, there is plenty else to occupy my thoughts, and one of those things is the fact that my daughter has been in a terrible mood since we got back from America, and even though I'm not at fault, she seems to blame me for what's happened. As she put it so succinctly at the airport before we flew back, she thinks that I am 'happy' now because my helping her to catch Daryl in a lie has ensured that she won't be moving over there to be with him and thus, leaving me over here by myself. But while I can't lie and say I wouldn't have missed her terribly if she had departed the UK permanently, there is no way I can be happy when she is so unhappy.

And unhappy she most certainly is.

Ellie has barely left her bedroom since we got back home, which isn't too much of a change since before America, but it's even more extreme this time. She is refusing to tell her friends that she is back, just like she is not going to go back to her restaurant job. But I'm more bothered about her not wanting to see her friends because for her to have no desire to hang out with them tells me that she feels embarrassed about what has happened, and she doesn't want them to laugh at her for chasing a crazy dream all the way to California only to return home with a broken heart and her tail between her legs.

I've tried to tell Ellie on several occasions that her friends will support her rather than take pleasure in her disappointment, but she won't listen, and I've done well just to get a few words out of my mouth before she has screamed at me to get out of her room again. So, after all this, it seems that things with my daughter are not even back at square one again but actually worse than they have ever been before. I tried to do my best by supporting her relationship with Daryl, but I couldn't ignore the photo and Daryl's lies surrounding Aubree, nor Harvey's ownership of a deadly weapon when he told me he didn't have it, and in the end, I had to do what a mother should do and that was make sure my daughter was safe. Now she is, though, she hates my guts, so I'm stopping short of calling it a complete victory just yet.

If all that wasn't enough trouble to keep one very tired and jetlagged woman worrying long into the night, there is a third thing that is bothering me and stopping my mind from being at ease, and it is potentially the most important reason of all.

It's the fact that, as of yet, I have not contacted the LAPD and passed on the information that Daryl was not only close to Aubree in the months before she went missing but has eminently denied that being the case when questioned about it. It warrants investigation and certainly because it seems the police have absolutely nothing else to go on at this time, which their fruitless search so far has proven. All it would take is one phone call, one anonymous tip-off, and a police car would drive over to Harvey's house, and a couple of officers would ring his doorbell. Then, after asking to come inside, they would not only ask Daryl what his relationship with Aubree was, but they would ask to see the photo in the box in the basement. Then, depending on what Daryl or, indeed, Harvey has to hide, they might get some answers. Maybe they will be shown the photo but if

Daryl denies its existence, I could always forward on the photo I have of it on my phone, although I'd hope I wouldn't have to because I don't want anyone knowing I'd be involved.

From there, it would be up to the police to decide what to do next.

So why haven't I done it? Why haven't I made the call and sent the police to their house to do a little investigating? Why am I keeping quiet about it?

It's quite simple, really.

It's because I promised Ellie on the plane home that I would drop it.

She doesn't care if Daryl is guilty or not, but in reality, I just think she doesn't want to know. It's one thing to know she was dating a serial liar but it's quite another to know she was seeing a guy who turned out to be a killer. I can understand why she thinks it's better not to open that can of worms, but I can also see it from another side too. I can see it from the side of Aubree's parents and how they are still hopelessly waiting by the phone for answers so long after their daughter vanished into thin air. If that was me, then I would want to know what happened to my child, even if it turned out to be something terrible, so if I can help those people, then why shouldn't I?

But doing that would mean breaking my promise to my daughter.

So, which is it to be?

It takes me until the end of my first night shift back at the supermarket before I make up my mind, and as I step outside the warehouse and witness the dawning of a new day, I realise what I have to do. Seeing this sunrise takes me back to the sunrise I witnessed in the desert as Harvey was driving me out there to try and find Daryl and Ellie, and it reminds me of the fear and panic I felt when I was afraid something bad had happened to my daughter amongst the barren landscape. Okay, so she turned out to be just fine when we found her, but there was a brief moment of anxiety that I had let my daughter be taken away into a dangerous situation from which I would never be able to see her again. That is not something any parent wants to experience, and fortunately, most parents on this planet never have to go through something like that. But Aubree's parents have, and right now, at this very moment in LA, they are still going through it.

The worrying for them has not ended yet.

But maybe I can do something to help that.

Taking out my phone, I try not to worry too much about what this overseas call is going to cost me, and as I hold my mobile to my ear, I wait to be connected to an operator for the Los Angeles Police Department. When I am, I decide that I am not going to give them my name or say where I am calling from, only that I have some information that might be useful towards an active investigation.

Then I give it to them.

I give them Daryl's name and his address, as well as the name of the missing person he is connected to and how there is a photo in his basement that proves me right.

And then I hang up before I can say anything more.

It's a matter for the police now.

Will they take me seriously and go and talk to Daryl, potentially resulting in the solving of a case that currently puzzles everyone?

Or have I just made a very stupid mistake?

30

ELLIE

I wake up to the sound of my mobile phone buzzing away on my bedside table and when I pick it up, I see that it is my best friend, Charlotte, trying to call me. But just like all her other calls recently, I ignore it and leave her unanswered. But I know she'll try again, and sure enough, she does.

Rolling over, I wrap my pillow around my head to drown out the sound of my incessant phone vibrating, but even as I reduce the sound of it, I know this is not a long-term strategy that can work.

The problem is that all my friends know I'm back home early from America.

Stacey, one of the girls I occasionally hang around with, lives at the end of my street and must have seen me arriving back the other day with Mum and all our luggage. She must have then passed that information on to Charlotte and the rest of our friends, and now the secret is out.

I'm back home before I should be, which means they all want to know one thing.

What happened?

But I'm nowhere near ready enough to face them and their questions, so I have been successfully avoiding them so far. But that hasn't stopped them from calling and texting me, and it's as if nothing exciting is going on in their world, so they have to know all about my drama to get them through the day. But of course, they do because nothing ever happens around here, so this is the most interesting thing that has happened lately. But screw them. I don't have to tell them what happened if I don't want to, nor do I accept their pity or sympathy or their invites to go out in town to a nightclub and find me a new boyfriend. I just want them all to leave me alone, just like I want my mum to leave me alone too.

She's already back at work, and while I do feel bad that she has accumulated debt from the trip to LA, I feel way worse than she must do. I've been lied to by somebody I love and lost the chance of a very exciting future, and now I'm back in this damn bedroom feeling sorry for myself, just like I have been for most of the last few years.

Life sucks, or at least mine does.

But at least I get a little respite when I remove the pillow from around my ears and realise that my phone is no longer being called. That's something, I suppose, but when I pick up my mobile, I see a text message that quickly puts an end to my brief moment of peace. It's a message from Charlotte and when I read it, it causes me to sit bolt-upright in my bed and almost have a heart attack.

I've just seen the news. Daryl has been arrested in LA! What the hell! It's him, right? Your boyfriend? Is this why you came back early? Omg Ellie, you have to call me! Xx

I can't believe what I'm reading and have no choice but to return Charlotte's calls to get some answers.

'Hey! Are you okay?' my friend asks me when she answers, but there's no time for pleasantries.

'What are you talking about? Daryl's been arrested?' I ask her.

'Yeah, I thought you would have known. Isn't that why you came back?'

'No! What's happened?'

'I heard you had come back early, but when you weren't answering me, I had a look on yours and Daryl's social media accounts. I saw somebody had posted something ten minutes ago to his Facebook profile telling him that they knew he was innocent and that he had to stay strong.'

'What?'

'Yeah, it's crazy, right? So I put his name into Google, and guess what? There are loads of articles about him being questioned by the police over some missing woman! What the hell is all that about?'

It's very rude of me, but I end the call without saying another word to Charlotte, but only because I need time to go online and read some of these articles myself. When I do, I find exactly what she said, which is dozens of links to news stories about there suddenly being a new suspect in the disappearance of Aubree.

Clicking the first one, I am taken onto an American news site that not only shows a photo of Daryl but talks about him being questioned over his relationship with the missing woman. The article doesn't mention that he has been charged with anything yet, only that he is a person of interest, but even so, this is crazy, and most of all, this is not supposed to be happening.

Unless…

I realise then that Mum must have broken her promise to me and contacted the LAPD. How else would they have known to go and talk to Daryl? This is her fault, and I can't believe she would do this. But the damage is seemingly done now, and everyone is looking at Daryl, which means everyone in this town is going to be looking at me, too, once they find out that I am his girlfriend.

I guess I technically still am because I haven't officially ended things with him yet since I got back home. He's sent me a few text messages, and I've replied to him, keeping things short and just telling him that I'm feeling sad and helping the family get ready for the funeral of my fictitious aunt Maggie. I know I should have just been honest with him by now and told him that I think he was lying to me and that we are over because the trust is ruined, but I haven't done it yet. Besides, he wasn't truthful with me, so there's no rush for me to be truthful with him.

But I was not expecting something like this to happen.

If Mum was here now, then I would scream and shout at her, but she isn't. She's at work, but she should be home soon, so I'll get my chance then. In the meantime, all I can do is read more of these articles online, as well as a few of the comments that members of the public have left underneath them all.

When I do see the comments, it's obvious that some people have already made their minds up and are calling Daryl guilty.

If he's done this, then he deserves to rot in hell!

Was Daryl her boyfriend? Scumbag!

I can't believe it's taken this long for the police to find out he was involved with her. What have they been doing all this time?

But there are a few other people who are reserving judgement until they know more facts.

Innocent until proven guilty!

I knew Daryl at university, and he would never hurt a fly!

This is nonsense! The truth will come out in the end, and I hope some of you people apologise when it does!

I guess some of these people know Daryl personally and are defending him, which is understandable, I suppose. But who is right here? Those who trust him or those who already think he's guilty?

Even though it would be horrendous if it turned out that he was the person who caused Aubree to go missing, part of me almost hopes he is guilty because at least then all of this won't have been for nothing. It seems almost worse to think of him being entirely innocent and subjected to all this media attention now if he hasn't done anything wrong. But what if he is innocent, and what if this is all my fault?

But it's not my fault if he is. It's Mum's fault, and when I hear her key in the front door downstairs, I jump out of bed and race down to meet her.

'What the hell have you done?' I cry at her before she's barely got inside the house.

She looks stunned at my sudden appearance, but after I've thrust my phone into her hand and forced her to read the article on the screen, she understands exactly why I am so mad at her.

So what does she say to that? What is her defence?

Does she apologise and say she regrets it? Does she even try and deny being involved, even though that would be a total lie that I would easily see through?

And does she beg for my forgiveness and tell me that she was just doing what she thought was best?

No, she doesn't do any of those things.

All Mum does is hand me back my phone and close the front door. Then, after taking a deep breath, she tells me that whatever is meant to be will be.

31

DAWN

Eating alone is not much fun but something I've sadly had a lot of practise at, thanks to two reasons.

One, losing my partner before his time.

And two, because my daughter has spent most of the last few years mad at me for various causes.

It's that second reason why I'm sitting alone on my sofa in front of my laptop, with a microwave meal on a tray and a solitary glass of water sitting on the coffee table beside me. This food tastes bland, as does my unimaginative drink, but one thing that can't be called boring is the personality of the American news reporter on the screen in front of me.

He's a hyped up, passionate man in a smart suit who is excitedly telling the viewers all about the latest news stories to hit the headlines in the United States, and while it took me a while to find this website online, once I did, I've been streaming the live feed constantly. That's because I'm eager to be kept up to date with what is going on with Daryl across the Atlantic.

I knew that my phone call to the LAPD was going to send out a ripple effect, but I had no idea that it was going to make headline news so quickly in America. I just presumed the police would quietly speak to Daryl, and even if they started to think he might have had something to do with Aubree going missing, I thought it would take a long time before it became public knowledge. But it seems that the media are all over any new developments in the case, which is why I came home to Ellie going mad at me about her boyfriend being in the news.

I feel so bad for breaking my promise to her, but as I tried to explain once she had calmed down a little bit, I had no choice because I would never have been able to forgive myself if it turned out I could have helped two desperate parents get answers. But despite that, Ellie has continued to tell me that I shouldn't have done this because if Daryl is innocent, then I might have just ruined his life.

I doubt that is the case because if he is innocent, then I'm sure all the attention around him will die down quickly enough, and the journalists in America will soon find somebody else to sink their teeth into. But what if he isn't innocent? Sure, this firestorm in the American media won't die down quickly then but why should it if Daryl did hurt Aubree? If he is guilty, then he deserves everything that is coming to him and more and not only that, but I will have saved my daughter from danger herself.

Chewing my tasteless meal as I keep watching the news, I hear the report talk about various other stories that hold no interest to me, like tales of financial corruption in New York and some scandal involving a politician in Wyoming. But I know that the case of the missing woman will be discussed shortly because it's all over the news online, and based on how many posters I saw showing Aubree's face while I was in Los Angeles, I know it will be the talk of that city too.

But as the reporter cuts to a commercial break, I am forced to wait a little longer to find out if there have been any more developments in Daryl's situation. Is he still being questioned? Has he been charged with anything yet? Or have the police let him go after he has proven to them that he couldn't have had anything to do with it?

While the answers to those questions will shape the rest of Daryl and Harvey's life, I have a feeling they will also shape the rest of mine and Ellie's too.

Either she is going to see that I was right to worry and forgive me.

Or she will find out that I was totally off the mark and then hate me forever.

I've got a 50/50 chance of my daughter loving me in the future.

With that in mind, I'm going to need something stronger to drink tonight than this damn tap water.

But just before I can put my plate down and go into the kitchen to get a more suitable drink for my mental state, the news comes back on and when it does, the reporter seems even more hyped up than he was before he went off air. That's because he has some breaking news to report and when I see what it is, I am glad I am sitting down because if I wasn't, then I would most certainly lose my balance and fall over.

Arrest made in the case of Aubree Parker says the rolling information bar at the bottom of the screen, and while the reporter excitedly tells the viewers that a suspect has been taken into custody, I am expecting them to talk about Daryl and how they uncovered the vital piece of evidence that proved he was to blame for this after all. But that doesn't happen. Instead, the camera cuts to footage outside a Los Angeles police station, and as I see a huge media scrum surrounding several police officers, I realise who is right in the middle of it all.

It's a man in handcuffs.

But it's not Daryl in custody.

It's Harvey.

As the father is put into the back of a police van and driven away from the station to be taken to a more secure premises, the reporter explains why he is now the one in trouble rather than his son.

It's because the truth has just come out, though it is not a truth I or anybody else was expecting.

Harvey has just admitted to killing Aubree.

32

ELLIE

I didn't need Mum to come bursting into my bedroom to tell me the shocking news because I'd already heard about it myself. But unlike her, I hadn't gotten my update from some impersonal news reader on some obscure American channel streamed over the internet. I'd actually gotten it from a very close source, the kind of source every journalist in LA wishes they had access to at present.

I got the news from Daryl.

It arrived in the form of a text message to my phone, and when I read it, I could not believe what it said. First of all, Daryl told me that he was sorry because he had lied to me about Aubree. He admitted then that he had been much closer to her than he had led me to believe, and he regretted not just being honest with me. But all of that was just a precursor to what he told me next.

He told me that his dad had admitted to killing her, and he didn't know how to handle this.

I'd just been about to call him when Mum had entered my bedroom and grabbed my laptop before showing me a video on a news website, which was a looped recording of a handcuffed Harvey being put into the back of a police van and transported somewhere. I didn't keep my attention on the laptop for long though. That was because I wanted to speak to Daryl as quickly as possible and find out if he was okay.

The thing was, I didn't want Mum to know that I was about to contact him, so I had to pretend to be surprised at the news she was showing me before listening to her say that she knew there was something weird about that family, but she had never imagined it could be this.

But a time like this is not the time for saying, 'I told you so,' so I expressed to Mum that I needed to be alone to think about this, and when she saw that I was upset, she thankfully left me in peace. But I wasn't upset because Mum was right and it turned out we had escaped what could have been a very dangerous situation over in LA. I was upset because despite what his evil father has done, Daryl is entirely innocent and now, with his dad in custody and his mum dead, he has absolutely no one.

No one except me.

I've been trying his phone several times since I saw his message, but so far, he hasn't answered me. But I'm not going to stop trying because I want to make sure that he is okay, if it's even possible for him to feel okay at this time, which it might not be.

How can he be handling the fact that his dad, the man he lives with and the only parent he has in this world now, has just admitted to being behind the disappearance of Aubree? He can't be taking it well. It's like me finding out Mum had done something terrible. I might have my disagreements with her but at the end of the day, I know she'll always be around for me. But imagine if she wasn't because she'd been arrested? What would I do then?

I'd feel totally and hopelessly lost.

With Daryl not answering his phone, I send him several messages, hoping that he will at least read one of them and see that I care about him and just want to make sure that he is okay. But so far, they are all going unread, so I have no idea if he is even looking at his phone now. Maybe he is having to talk to the police again, or maybe he has managed to get a moment with Harvey where he can ask his dad what the hell is going on. Or maybe he has just locked himself away in a room somewhere, trying to escape all the journalists that are desperate to get him on camera and ask him if his father is a killer.

At the moment, all Harvey seems to have done is admit that he killed Aubree, but no more details have come out. I guess it depends on how much he is actually going to say to the police whether or not any more information is forthcoming in the next few days. If he doesn't give them the full story, then I guess there will just have to be a big investigation and maybe even a trial, and the thought of Harvey being at the centre of the biggest news story in America is just insane to me.

It's not that long ago that I was at his house, swimming in his pool, eating his food and being driven around in his car. Back then, he just seemed like a normal guy and no different to the father of any of the other guys I've dated in the past. He was polite but awkward, clearly anxious to make a good impression on me for the sake of his son, and while some of his attempts at humour fell flat, I could tell that he was just trying hard to get me to like him. Very normal, very average and really, I paid far less attention to him than I did to Daryl because I wasn't there for Harvey; I was there for his son. But it turns out

Harvey was so much more than what he showed to me and Mum. He had another side to him, one neither of us could have imagined, and I doubt anyone who knew him even better than we did could have imagined it.

Surely Daryl couldn't either.

Mum makes several more attempts to come into my bedroom and talk to me as the night goes on, but I manage to repel most of them by telling her that I just need more time to process all of this and don't really want to talk about any of it at the moment. But really, I am just saying that because I want to keep myself free in case Daryl should call me because I never know if and when he might actually do that.

And then, just after midnight UK time, my phone starts ringing, and I see that it is him.

'Daryl? Are you okay? What's going on?' I ask him, bombarding him with questions from the first second the call connects because I don't know how long he is going to stay on the phone for, so I need him to know that I care before he goes again. But he doesn't hang up or seem to be in any kind of a rush to get off the phone. Instead, he is very quiet, but as I listen down the line, I hear what sounds like him crying all the way over there in America.

'Daryl! What's going on? Just tell me! I'm here for you!' I say, my voice getting way too loud for this time of night, and sure enough, Mum has heard me and is making her way towards my bedroom. But even though she is about to come in, I know she won't be able to hear what Daryl is saying, so I'm not too bothered about her interrupting.

'It's my dad,' Daryl says quietly in between sobs.

'I know,' I say, my heart breaking for him. 'What's happened? What has he done?'

My bedroom door opens then, and Mum appears, and when she sees me on the phone, she mouths to me, 'Who is that?' But when I don't answer, she speaks louder this time and asks me directly if it is Daryl.

I nod my head at her but put out a hand to tell her to keep her distance until I have heard what he has got to say, and thankfully, she mostly does that, although she does creep a little closer, no doubt hoping to hear some of the words coming from the other end of the phone. But I doubt she can because I can barely hear Daryl as it is, even with my ear pressed as tightly as possible to my device, and that's because the caller is still being very quiet.

'I think he killed her,' Daryl says meekly.

'I don't understand.'

Mum sees the shock register on my face and asks me what I just heard, but I turn away from her and ask Daryl for more information.

'Has he said why?' I ask, and Daryl is quiet for several seconds before answering me.

'I'm not sure. I only know what I've been told by the police. He's admitted to her murder, and now he is taking them to…'

Daryl's sentence trails off then, and he is full on crying now, so I give him a little time before I ask him where Harvey is taking the police to. But when he tells me, my body turns cold.

'He's taking them to where he buried her,' comes the frightened, confused response.

33

DAWN

I just cannot believe this. This man who I sat and drank wine with, who I shared intimate feelings about being a widow with and the man who was the father of my daughter's boyfriend, is a killer.

I feel sick just thinking about it for many reasons, not least of which because there were at least two occasions during my time with Harvey when I actually felt like we had a moment, and he was hinting that perhaps something could happen between the two of us. At the time, I just thought it was because he was lonely or drunk, but what if he was trying to get closer to me?

What if he had nefarious plans for me like he did with Aubree?

But this isn't just about me. It's about everybody else caught up in this horrendous situation. Of course, there is Ellie, the person that matters most to me, and it's hard to see her so shell-shocked by this turn of events. Right now, my primary focus is on making sure she is okay. But this is also about Daryl too, the person I was initially suspicious of but someone who is more a victim than a suspect, and now I feel guilty for thinking badly of him when he's done nothing wrong.

He's been so let down by his father, and my heart breaks for him and all he is having to deal with over there in Los Angeles. And then, of course, there is Aubree's family. Their dream of her suddenly walking through their front door and letting them know that she is okay has died, and while they still don't have the full story yet, or even a body to move towards closure with, things are never going to be the same for them whatever happens from here.

It's been twenty-four hours since I first found out that Harvey had been arrested, and a lot has happened since then. It started with me hearing Ellie on the phone to Daryl and asking her what he was saying. She didn't tell me until she had gotten off the call but when she did, it sounded utterly horrendous. Apparently, Harvey had admitted to the murder and was on his way with the police to her burial site. As if that wasn't crazy enough, Ellie and I were able to watch actual live footage of that very grim voyage online because several U.S. news channels had helicopters in the air and had followed the procession of police cars out of Los Angeles and into the desert where Harvey was instructing the authorities to go.

To me, the scene was not particularly recognisable or significant as I watched the bird's eye view of several police vehicles driving down a desert highway before turning off onto a dirt track and heading into the mountains. But it became a lot more personal when I realised exactly where they had stopped at.

It was the same place Daryl had taken Ellie to see the sunrise and the same place Harvey had driven me to when we were trying to find them.

That fact had not been lost on my daughter either, and once she realised where it was, she had immediately tried to contact Daryl again. But he hadn't answered his phone, so all we had to go off was what we were watching over the internet, and as we kept our eyes on the screen like some morbid voyeuristic viewers, we were witnesses at the exact moment the news came through that a body had been discovered in the location on the screen.

I hadn't realised it at the time because I had been so engrossed in what I was watching, but the sun had risen outside our house, and Ellie and I had been up the entire night watching events in California. But by the time the sun was beginning to set on another summer's day on the west coast of America, it seemed Aubree's family finally had the thing they had been searching for for so long.

They finally had the location of their missing daughter.

Ellie and I had continued to gawk at the news channels for further updates, fuelling ourselves through our marathon watch by drinking coffee, although we stopped well short of getting any snacks out of the cupboard. Somehow, this was not quite the right occasion for popcorn or chocolate, not that either of us had much of an appetite anyway, thanks to what we were watching and how close to home it felt to us.

Despite this being thousands of miles away, Ellie and I not only knew the man in custody, but had also been to the place he had buried his victim, and while we knew that, I wondered how long it was going to take before some of the journalists in this country knew that too. If they did figure it out, and a little gossip from some of mine and Ellie's friends might be all they needed to get a tip-off, then they would surely descend on this quiet street and be desperate to stick a microphone in our faces to get our side of the story about our time spent in America with a now notorious killer. But thankfully, so far, nobody from the British media has come to our house and tried to bother us.

But I think it's only a matter of time until they do because it's not often a mother and daughter in sleepy Suffolk have a connection to a famous killer in California, and I can already imagine a few of the headlines before they have been written.

Englishwoman's American boyfriend and his killer dad!

Lucky escape in LA for British pair!

The daughter, the boyfriend, the mother and the murderer!

I can't comprehend or bear the thought of Ellie's name and face splashed all over the newspapers, never mind my own, and I can only hope that it doesn't come to that. But that is probably me being very optimistic, and right now, that's about the only thing I can be scarcely optimistic about. That's because as the news keeps coming, things only get grimmer.

The entire life story of Harvey and his family is currently being played out in the media; reporters, journalists and seemingly anybody with access to a camera or a social media account are discussing the man and his loved ones with impunity. Anybody watching these news channels is hearing all about Harvey and where he lived, where he worked and even which supermarket he shopped in. That last part is thanks to a segment featuring some old lady talking to a reporter in which she said how she used to see Harvey buying groceries every week and always thought he seemed like a nice man.

Pulitzer Prize winning stuff.

Digging deeper, the media know that Harvey is a widower and give the background story of him losing his wife, with some then speculating that such a thing might have been the catalyst for him to lose his grip on reality and go from law-abiding citizen to national hate figure and soon-to-be convicted killer. Then they quickly move on to Daryl, making sure to mention that Harvey's son was initially a suspect in Aubree's disappearance but now is just yet another victim in this terribly sad story. Daryl's personal life is delved into as much as Harvey's is, including which school he went to, where he currently works, but thankfully, as of yet, there is no mention of him having been in a relationship with Ellie.

But there is mention of the fact that Daryl was close to Aubree, and I gasp when I see a photo on screen that I recognise very well. It's the photo I saw in the basement at Harvey's house, the one of Daryl with his arm around Aubree beside his father's pool, and I guess it was discovered during a search of the property once the investigation really ramped up. From that, and just like I did, the police and the media now know that the murdered woman was linked to this family, and while no exact motive on Harvey's part has been offered up to the authorities, it hasn't stopped everybody who is interested in this case speculating about it. Apparently, Twitter is rife with theories, but at the moment, that is all they are.

I guess none of us will really know what happened unless Harvey decides to enlighten us.

Thankfully, but shockingly, he was very close to doing just that.

34

ELLIE

In the end, I had to tell Mum to turn the news off because I couldn't bear to watch it anymore. Now we're both in bed trying to get some long overdue sleep after staying up all night to follow events in LA, though I almost wish I hadn't. Watching and hearing about all those things means I can't sleep now, and every time I close my eyes, I either see Daryl crying, Harvey in handcuffs or my imagination conjuring up an image of Aubree lying in a shallow grave in the desert, surrounded by police officers, forensic experts and detectives.

What a horrible mess, and it's so bad that I'm even contemplating something that Mum suggested to me a while ago, something I never thought I would do.

Counselling.

She's always tried to get me to go and speak to somebody ever since Dad died, not just as a way to process my grief but as a way to focus on my future and figure out what I want to do with my life. I've never been interested, but strangely enough, as I lie here thinking about a dead body and how I hugged a killer before staying at his house, I could do with getting a few things off my chest. But I'm far too exhausted to do anything about it now, though I might just mention it to Mum in the next few days, and I'm sure she'll be pleased when I tell her I want to open up to somebody.

But I wish Daryl would open up to me, too, at this time. I've not stopped texting him throughout the night while I was sitting with Mum watching the news, and while he hasn't always been quick to reply, he has come back a few times. But he's being very vague, and I just know he's holding his real thoughts and feelings in, possibly embarrassed at crying over the phone earlier and not wanting to be so emotional with me again. But he can be however he wants to be with me because I just want him to know that I am here for him and that I love him regardless of what his father has done.

That's right, I love him.

I don't need to pick up my pen and write in my diary to process my internal thoughts anymore because I am crystal clear on this one thing. I want to get back with Daryl and be together again like we were before all this craziness started. I always regretted leaving him so suddenly but felt I had no choice when I found out he was lying to me. But things have changed a lot since then, and while he might not be perfect, he's a much better man than his father has turned out to be, and most of all, I might be all he has left.

I don't know what will happen to Daryl now his dad is likely going to prison for the rest of his life. I presume the house will be sold, so where will he live then? Will he get the money from the sale so he can set himself up again, or will it go to his father, or will the government take it because they don't want a criminal to profit off a lucrative land sale? I have no idea, but what I do know is that Daryl doesn't have much other family in LA, so where will he go? A friend's place? Maybe, if they'll have him, but that's not very long-term. What if he is too embarrassed to ask for help and ends up on the streets? What if the horror of what his father has done is too much for him and he starts drinking or taking drugs and ends up dying of an overdose under some bridge in a dangerous part of the city?

What if I lose him and never get to see him again?

Not wanting to go another second of imagining Daryl on the verge of a complete breakdown all the way over there in California, I send him a very quick and simple message.

If you want to, you can come and stay here with me. We can get through this together. I love you xx

I've extended that invitation without consulting Mum but surely, I don't need to. She can't object to it, can she? How heartless would it be of her to say no and leave a poor young man all by himself after what he's been through with both of his parents? She's not a monster, not like Harvey. She has a heart, and she will just want to help Daryl like I do.

But will Daryl accept my offer?

I get no response for a while, and the next thing I know, I'm waking up three hours later, surprising myself that I managed to drift off to sleep, but I guess I simply got too exhausted to keep my eyes open in the end. But when I wake up, I see a missed call from Daryl twelve minutes ago, so I try him, and he answers me straight away.

I'm wondering if he is calling me because he wants to discuss my idea of him coming to stay with me.

But before he even mentions that, he has more information about his dad.

More specifically, his dad's motives for doing what he did.

35

ELLIE

'Sorry for not replying to your messages for a while,' Daryl begins, his voice still meek and sounding even further away than our distance would suggest. 'I've been talking to the police for hours.'

'Why? You're not still a suspect, are you?'

'No, of course not. Dad did this, not me. But now I know why. The police have been telling me what he has told them.'

'And?'

Daryl lets out a very heavy sigh before continuing but when he does, he has another apology to offer me first.

'Like I said, I did know Aubree a little more than I told you, and I'm sorry about that. The thing is, I hadn't seen her since school, but I bumped into her one day three months ago when I was on the way home from work. We got chatting, and there was a little flirting. It was a really hot day, and she said she was going to go to the beach. But the beach was quite far, and I have a pool at my place, so I suggested she come for a swim at mine. I know it was a little fast, but like I said, we were flirting, it was a very hot day, and we did kind of know each other from school, even though it was a long time ago.'

'Okay, so what happened?' I ask, wondering how it got from an invitation to use the pool to Harvey showing the police where a body was buried.

'We went back home and got in the pool,' Daryl tells me, an innocent lilt to his voice, but it only makes me feel sad because I know that while this story might have started innocently enough, it certainly does not end that way. 'We were just chilling, having a drink, chatting about school and who we still talked to from back then. If I'm honest, I was kind of thinking about making a move on her at some point, but then Dad came home and interrupted us.'

I daren't ask what happened next, but it can't be good, so I just keep listening.

'At first, I thought he might be mad that I'd brought someone to the house without asking him,' Daryl says, his voice a little louder and clearer now than it was when this call first started. 'But he was fine with it and seemed happy when I told him Aubree was someone from school. He offered to make us some nachos and went inside to get us another drink. I guess he was happy I was with someone because I hadn't really made much effort with people since Mum died.'

I know exactly what he means but say nothing again.

'We got out of the pool for the nachos, and Dad offered to take a photo of the two of us, which I thought was a little weird because I hadn't asked him to do that. But he took it, and that's the photo you might have seen on the news.'

I tell him that I have seen it, although I don't mention that I actually saw it much earlier than that when Mum found it in his basement.

'So what happened?' I ask, impatient to know how things suddenly went so wrong.

'Not much, really. We had the nachos and a couple more drinks, and then the sun was going down, so Aubree said she had to get going. I couldn't drive her, though, because I'd had too much to drink, so Dad offered, but she said no. Apparently, she was going to go and see a friend who lived nearby, so she was happy to walk. I mean, it's a safe neighbourhood, so that didn't seem like a big deal, so I showed her out and said we'd have to do it again sometime before she left. That was it.'

'What do you mean that was it?'

'I never saw her again. The next thing I heard, she was on the news because her parents had reported her missing.'

'She went missing that night?'

'Yeah.'

Daryl sounds very quiet again now, and it's no doubt because he feels guilty that she might have been okay if she hadn't come to his house that day.

'I don't understand,' I say, confused. 'If she was okay when she left, how did your dad hurt her?'

'That's the thing. I had no idea until a police officer told me a couple of hours ago.'

Daryl starts sobbing then, and I suddenly fear he's going to hang up and I'll lose him before I get the full story, so I tell him it's okay and that he can talk to me.

Thankfully, he stays on the line, and after he's regained his composure, he starts talking again.

'Dad has told the police that he left the house that night shortly after Aubree had gone. He must have done it while I was upstairs in the shower. That's what I went to do just after I said goodbye to her.'

'He followed her?' I ask, and Daryl says so.

'He's told the police that he was attracted to Aubree when he saw her, and because he was so lonely since Mum, he couldn't help himself. He'd had a few drinks when he got home and caught up with her on the street, and because he knew she'd had a few drinks too, he apparently tried to kiss her.'

'What?'

'I know, it's insane,' Daryl says, his voice a mixture of shock, disgust and disbelief. 'She's like half his age.'

'What happened?'

'He said she rejected him and told him to leave her alone. But he didn't do that and tried to pull her towards him. They had a scuffle, and as she was trying to get away, he lost his grip on her, and she fell back and hit her head on the pavement.'

I put my hand to my mouth to stop myself from gasping as I listen to this horrible story.

'Dad said he panicked then because she didn't get back up, and when he tried to move her, she was limp.'

'No,' is all I can utter, feeling sick to my stomach.

'The police told me he confessed to dragging her body into some bushes, so it was hidden, then ran back to get his car. I remember him coming upstairs when I'd got out of the shower and telling me he had to go and pick up a few groceries that he'd forgotten to get earlier. He was always forgetting stuff since Mum died, so I didn't think it was weird. Then he went out. But I guess he wasn't going to the supermarket. He was moving Aubree's body.'

Now I actually feel like I could be sick.

'He drove her out to the desert and buried her?' I ask, even though it's less of a question and more of a statement of fact at this point.

'Yeah,' Daryl replies quietly. 'But it's where he buried her that's the worst part of all this.'

'I know. It's the place you took me to watch the sunrise,' I say.

'Yeah, but that's not all it is,' Daryl interjects before I can say anything else. 'Remember that clearing I took you to in between all the rocks? The one I said was special.'

'Yeah.'

'We got interrupted before I could tell you why it was so special. It's because that was the place where Dad told me he proposed to Mum before I was born. That was where she said yes to marrying him. That's how I knew about that place. I'd been there several times as a kid with Mum and Dad, and that's why I liked to go back so much after Mum had died.'

My heart is breaking for Daryl, and I don't even need him to say the last part of the story, but he says it anyway.

'Dad buried Aubree in the same spot he proposed to Mum,' he tells me, anger now coming through in his voice. 'I guess he knew hardly anybody went there, so it was unlikely anybody would find her.'

I shake my head at what I'm hearing, but as Daryl and I share a moment of stunned silence over the phone, I have to know one more thing.

'Why did your dad confess to this?' I ask Daryl, but then, the answer is an obvious one.

'Because I was being questioned about it. He'd made me stay quiet about Aubree being at our house the night she went missing because he said the police would make me a prime suspect if they knew about it. I just thought he was protecting me and figured the cops would catch whoever had really done it. But when they came to question me, I assumed they had found out she was at my place, so I told them the truth about her coming to use our pool. But then Dad must have panicked that they were close to figuring out Aubree had died around here, so rather than risk me getting in trouble for something I didn't do, he confessed to everything.'

It's then I realise that if Mum hadn't made that phone call to the police, then Harvey would most likely have gotten away with his crime, and Daryl would never have known what really happened to Aubree after she left his house that night.

But now the truth is out, what happens next?

Daryl and I spend the next hour on the phone discussing just that, and by the time we're done, I have to go and have a very serious conversation with Mum about the future.

36

DAWN

I'm back at the airport again, only this time I'm standing by the Arrivals sign rather than the one that says Departures. Ellie is beside me, and as we watch dozens of passengers emerging from deep within the airport and pouring out into this increasingly crowded area, the pair of us are keeping a look out for the traveller we have come here to meet.

Daryl.

The young man was on the flight that left America eleven hours ago, and he should be joining us here in England any minute now, though I needed much more than eleven hours to process the fact that he was coming here and how it would change my life when he arrived.

It was actually two months ago when Ellie first floated the idea of Daryl coming here to stay with us. At the time she did that, I and everybody else who was keeping abreast of the news was still reeling from the fact that Daryl's father had killed Aubree. The terrible timing of Ellie's request meant that I couldn't even consider it, and I told her emphatically that Daryl could not come here, not least because it would bring huge media attention upon us. But Ellie was persistent, as she always is, and over the course of the next few weeks, she stated her case for why Daryl should come to stay with us.

'He doesn't have anybody else.'

'Don't you feel sorry for him? We need to help him.'

'I love him and want to make sure he is okay.'

'Have a heart. How would you feel if I was all alone and nobody was helping me?'

They were all things that Ellie said to me during our many discussions, and to be fair, they were all strong arguments. Of course I felt sorry for Daryl, and of course I had a heart. I also could see that Ellie was still very much in love with him, and considering it turned out that he was entirely innocent in all of this, I couldn't really tell her not to feel that way about him. But it was perhaps one of the last things she said to me before I made my decision that ultimately saw me give in and grant her her wish.

'If you don't let him come here to me, then I am going to go over there to him, and then you'll hardly ever see me.'

Ellie's statement, or thinly veiled threat as it was more like, made me see that she had made her mind up to be with Daryl, and there was nothing I could do about that other than decide where it was that she was with him.

Here.

Or America.

In the end, there was only one choice.

'Can you see him? I can't see him!' Ellie says as she strains her neck and stands on her tiptoes, trying to see over the heads of all the people in front of us as she scours the crowd for Daryl.

'He'll be coming out. Just relax,' I reply, but that seems a silly thing to say when my nerves are jangling as well. There are many reasons for my nervousness, not least of which is what it is going to be like to see and talk to Daryl again after what his father has done. It's bound to be very awkward and very difficult.

What do I do? Acknowledge the terrible subject straight away or avoid it entirely? I don't see how I can't not mention it, but I don't know how Daryl will react if I do. Start crying? Get angry? Is he depressed? In shock? At best, he must be traumatised, and Ellie has mentioned he has already had a few therapy sessions, but does he really need me talking to him about his killer dad too?

Not only is there that huge elephant in the room to deal with when he comes to stay with us, but there's also the fact that the media are bound to find out what's going on and try and get the scoop on it. So far, Ellie and I have managed to avoid saying anything to any journalist about Harvey, but that doesn't mean our photos haven't been taken and our names mentioned in the news.

As I feared, it didn't take long for somebody who knew us to sell their story to the newspapers, and I just hope the cash was worth it because they are no longer a friend of mine. The guilty party turned out to be Kirsty, my old work friend and one of the women who was part of my weekly coffee catch-up, but now, instead of there being four of us who go to that café for a chat, there are now only three because Kirsty is no longer welcome. I still wonder if she cares. Maybe, but then again maybe not, because the last I heard, she was having an extension built on her house, and I suspect all of that building work was paid for from the proceeds of selling her story to the national newspaper she had no qualms in talking to.

My Best Friend Lived With Killer Dad In America read the headline on the front page of the Sunday newspaper six weeks ago, almost causing me to vomit when I saw it before I angrily messaged the rest of my friends and told them that Kirsty was now dead to me. It wasn't just the fact that she had sold her story but shared several photos of me and her taken over the years, meaning my face was seen by millions of people more than it had to be. She also shared a photo of Sean, dragging my late partner into all this when he should be resting in peace.

'Where is he?' Ellie says again, growing more impatient by the second, and for a moment, I wonder if Daryl changed his mind and didn't get on the plane to come here. Maybe he suddenly decided to stay back in LA and be closer to some of the people he knew over there. But from what Ellie has told me, he couldn't wait to get away, and when I spot him making his way towards us through the throng of other weary passengers on his flight, I realise this is really happening.

Daryl is here, and pretty soon, he is going to be living in my house.

'There he is!' Ellie cries, and she abandons me to run towards her boyfriend.

When she reaches him, she almost knocks him over, such is her eagerness to wrap her arms around him and give him a tight hug. Daryl drops his suitcase as the pair of them squeeze each other before kissing, but I stop watching them because I want to scan this crowd to see if there are any journalists here taking photos and hoping to make this airport rendezvous a feature on tonight's evening news. But I can't see anybody watching my daughter and Daryl; however that might change very quickly if somebody recognises him or us from the news, so I hurry over to the besotted pair to tell them to get a move on.

'Hi, Daryl,' I say rather awkwardly when I greet the American, and from being this close to him, I can see a little of the toil the last couple of months have taken on him.

He has lost weight, and despite being in one of the sunniest cities on the planet, he is extremely pale, suggesting he has spent a lot of time indoors, and who can blame him? The media frenzy over there will have been on another scale to what it was over here.

Daryl smiles weakly at me before thanking me for allowing him to come here and see Ellie, and while I still have a few misgivings about all of this, I remember what this poor young man has been through and tell him not to worry about it. Then I suggest we head to my car quickly, and as Ellie and Daryl follow me, I lead them out of the airport to where I am parked.

The conversation during the drive back to my house is slightly stilted, if only because asking some of the usual questions I would ask to someone I hadn't seen for a while does not really feel appropriate.

What shall I say?

'How's it going, Daryl? Are you keeping well? Shame about what your dad did, but chin up, I'm sure things will get better for you soon.'

Yeah, somehow, asking Daryl how things have been for him recently is not something I want to do, so I just stay quiet as I drive back from the airport. Daryl is unsurprisingly quiet, too, definitely not as chatty and energetic as he was the first time I met him. But Ellie is doing her best to fill the awkward silences and rather expertly keeping a little conversation flowing without mentioning any tender topics.

She is busy telling Daryl about some of the places she is going to take him to see over here, much like how he was with her when we were in the car with him and Harvey after they collected us at LAX not so long ago. But while the three of us are still free to do what we want, Harvey is locked away in a cell and will remain there for the rest of his life.

I cannot imagine what he must be feeling like. There'll be no more swims in the pool for him or late-night bottles of wine, or trips to the beach. His life is ruined, though he only has himself to blame for that. But as for Daryl, while his life might be ruined also, he is not to blame, and maybe, given time, he can turn his life around and get back to being somewhat happy again. I guess I have a big part to play in that, just like Ellie, because now he is going to be living under my roof. I have no idea how long it is for, but Ellie has plans to help him get a job and then the two of them will supposedly look for somewhere else to live, a place of their own. But for now, the three of us are together, and as I park on my driveway, I remind myself that I am trying to do a good deed here.

But what's that famous saying for when a person tries to do the right thing only for it to backfire on them?

'No good deed goes unpunished.'

I can only hope that this good deed does not backfire on me and my family in a spectacular way.

37

ELLIE

It's been a week since Daryl got to England and all things considered, it's gone quite well.

I always knew his mood was going to be downbeat, but I've done my best to not only try and cheer him up, but allow him to have his vulnerable moments because it's important he doesn't bottle up his emotions and try to pretend like everything is okay. We've spent quite a bit of time in bed together, though it's all been watching movies, eating takeaway pizza and talking rather than anything physical. But I'm sure that will come in time, but for now, I don't want to rush Daryl and would rather he take more time to process what has happened with his dad.

Going out together was always going to be tricky, and I've been super paranoid that there would be journalists lurking in bushes ready to jump out at us and take our photo, but thankfully, that hasn't happened yet. We've been to the local park a couple of times for a walk during the middle part of the day when it's been fairly quiet with everyone around here at work, as well as been to the cinema to watch a few films because nobody is likely to recognise us in a dark room. But I've stopped short of taking Daryl into the centre of town or to any bustling shopping centres because that seems like too much of a risk, and we'd be inviting somebody spotting us, and then the stories in the news would start again.

Murderer's Son Secretly in Suffolk would likely be one of the many headlines if people knew Daryl was here. But so far, nobody knows. I haven't told any of my friends, and Mum has kept quiet about it too at her end, and I guess we'll just see how long we can keep it a secret for. I know it can't last forever, especially if Daryl decides to stay with me and we end up building a life together around here, but for now, we're just trying to focus on each other without any outside distractions.

Mum has been great with Daryl so far, not causing any problems for us, and while I know it must be weird for her to have my boyfriend living with us, she hasn't given him or me a hard time over it since he arrived. I think, just like me, she has seen how broken Daryl has been over what his dad has done and so knows it's unfair to punish him anymore.

I have asked Daryl a few times about whether or not he thinks he would ever go to visit his father in prison, but Daryl has told me it's far too early to think about anything like that. He did admit to going to see him once, though, not long after Harvey had confessed to everything, and he told me that was because he was refusing to believe the horrible story unless he heard it from his father himself. Alas, the story was confirmed, and Daryl left, and since then, he hasn't been back to see his dad, and I wonder if he ever will.

As for this evening, I'm currently lying on my bed trying to download a movie for the two of us to watch on my laptop when Daryl comes back from the bathroom and suggests that we go for a walk.

'It looks like a lovely night,' he says. 'How about we go to the park and watch the sunset?'

Knowing just how much Daryl likes all things to do with the sun coming up and going down, I can't say I'm surprised by his suggestion, though I'm not sure if I can be bothered to go out now I'm cosy. There's also the fact that Mum is at work, so I feel like it's quite nice for us to have the house to ourselves for a little while before she gets back. But Daryl seems eager to go, reminding me that summer won't last forever, and he's heard all about how dark and grim English winters can be, so we should make the most of a night like this while we still can. I can't argue with that, so I get up off the bed, and after I've packed a blanket, a bottle of wine from Mum's stash and a couple of packets of crisps, I say we are set for our picnic in the park.

The sky is a lovely orange as we leave the house and make our way towards the park, and I estimate we have about an hour left before the sun goes down completely and darkness falls. But we've got our jackets on, and it's a mild night, so we should be good for at least a couple of hours yet, though I must remember to text Mum at some point and tell her where we are because she'll finish her shift soon and won't be expecting the house to be empty when she gets back.

Daryl and I pass a few families on their way back from the park, kids on bicycles while the parents carry things like footballs and plastic toys under their arms, and Daryl pulls the brim of his baseball cap a little further down over his face as we cross the street and pass them. But once I am satisfied that he hasn't been recognised by any of the families, I entertain a more pleasant thought. While it's something way, way off in the future, I do wonder for a moment what it would be like if Daryl and I stayed together long enough to start a family of our own. But I'm definitely not going to let him know what I'm thinking about because I don't want to scare him off.

Play it cool, Ellie, I say to myself as we enter the park, and we find ourselves a quiet spot behind some trees, out of sight of anyone else in the park but somewhere with a great view of the continuing sunset that is unfolding before us.

But while I am reminding myself to take things slowly with Daryl, I am keen to see if he wants to be a little more intimate like we were in America, and so, after a little chatting and snacking on crisps, I wait until darkness has fallen and we're definitely the last two people in this park. Then I start to kiss him with the idea that we could take things a little further if we want to. I get that we're in a public place, but we're hidden away, and I feel more relaxed here than I would do at home, knowing Mum is only in the other room.

'Sorry,' Daryl says after we have been kissing for a couple of minutes, and my hands have started to wander down the t-shirt covering his torso. 'I'm just not ready yet.'

He moves my hands away before they get anywhere near his waist, but I don't feel annoyed or embarrassed, just sad for him and how he must still be feeling so hurt by his father that he can't even comprehend being more intimate with me like he once was before.

'That's okay,' I say, silently lamenting the fact that I let myself get carried away a little in the moment. 'I'm sorry. How about some more crisps?'

Daryl smiles at how quickly I have changed the subject, and as we lie back again and stare up at the dark sky, the memory of the beautiful sunset we just witnessed is still clear in our minds. But as I lie there, I have forgotten to do something I told myself I would do.

I haven't told Mum where I am.

She's probably home now and most likely wondering where we are, so I should reach into my bag and get my phone to send her a message. But just as I go to do that, Daryl apologises again for brushing me off a moment ago and says he wants to try again.

Not wanting to ruin the mood, I put my phone down before I've even looked at it and start kissing him once more.

Then I forget all about Mum again.

38

DAWN

I check my phone only to see that Ellie still hasn't replied to my message asking her where she is.
I know she's old enough to be out doing her own thing, but as she's living with me, she knows the rules. I appreciate it if she lets me know when she is coming and going at the house, so she knows better than this. But so far, she seems to have no interest in letting me know where she might have gone with Daryl.

I only got home ten minutes ago, so for the moment, getting something to eat after another draining shift is my priority, so I make myself yet another microwave meal and then settle down to eat it in front of the TV. Today's stint at the supermarket was a particularly gruelling one because we had a big delivery, and I had to help move some of the heavy stock thanks to two of my colleagues not being there because they had conveniently phoned in sick. *Whatever.* At least it's done with now, and I actually have a rare day off tomorrow, so I can relax tonight and try to unwind. But I can't totally relax until I know what Ellie is doing, so I keep checking my phone as I eat.
While I'm doing that, a fairly bland episode of some TV drama I haven't watched consistently for years is on in the background, and I'm only half paying attention to it. But my ears prick up when I hear one character say a line I've heard someone else say recently.
'I'd do anything for my son.'

The comment is made by the patriarchal mother in this particular television show, but the reason it gets my attention is because it reminds me of the last time I heard someone say that. It was Harvey who said that exact same thing while we were sitting by the pool late one night talking about our kids. He said he would do anything for Daryl, anything, and all that mattered was that he was safe.

Why has my stomach suddenly lurched as I recall that?

As I stop what I am doing and think about it some more, a terrifying thought occurs to me.

What if Harvey literally meant what he said? What if he really would do anything for his son?

Like take the blame for a crime his son actually committed.

It's a wild idea, but as my heart rate quickens, I think about whether or not it could be possible. Could Harvey actually be innocent and have given a false confession to the police just to stop them questioning Daryl? What if Daryl was the one who hurt Aubree but rather than let his son go to prison forever, Harvey has taken it upon himself to save his boy and let him live his life on the outside? What if that was why Harvey knew exactly where the body was buried? Not because he put it there, but because Daryl did, and when that secret was under threat, Harvey deflected all the attention off Daryl and onto him.

Having been around Harvey for a short while, it was obvious how much he loved his son, and considering he is a widower, I know what the thought of losing his child would do to him when he's all he had left.

Did Harvey decide that Daryl wouldn't survive prison so put himself in there in his place?

It's insane.

But could it be true?

The fact that I am now trying to call Ellie to speak to her tells me that I cannot afford to risk the alternative, but despite trying her again and again, she doesn't answer me, and that's when I feel the nausea return. It's the same nausea I felt when I realised Ellie had vanished with Daryl the first time because I hate not knowing where she is. Now she has disappeared with him again, I am afraid things aren't going to be as simple as last time. That's because, unlike then, I don't have Harvey to help me track them down.

I don't know where Ellie could be.

I also don't know if Daryl is really the person who killed Aubree.

But what if he is?

Is that why Daryl has come here?

Has he come to finish what he tried to start in America?

Is my daughter his next victim?

39

ELLIE

We're kissing now, and while I'm not sure what prompted Daryl to change his mind and want to be physical again, I'm glad it's happening because hopefully, it's a sign that things can start getting a bit more normal between us.

He's certainly more passionate this time than he was five minutes ago, and as he rolls over to be on top of me, I quite like the feeling of his body weight pressing down on me. But then something happens to spoil the moment slightly.

I move my arm to put it around Daryl's back but when I do, I accidentally knock over my bag, causing some of the items inside to spill out onto the grass beside our blanket. One of those items is my phone, and when I look at it, I see the screen lit up with several notifications.

'One second,' I say to Daryl after breaking off from his kiss, and I reach for my mobile. When I pick it up and bring it closer to my face, I see that all the notifications are from my mum. I have six missed calls and four new messages, and the latest one is very direct.

ANSWER YOUR PHONE! IT'S URGENT!

It's obvious to me then that I should not have neglected telling Mum where I was going because she's clearly angry at me. Unless this is about something else, and the fact she says urgent makes me worry something bad might have happened either to her or somebody we know.

'Sorry, I just need to call my mum,' I say to Daryl as he attempts to kiss my neck, but he's clearly not in the mood for any further interruptions.

'Leave it,' he tells me, and while I am seriously tempted to do as he says, the fact Mum used all capital letters in her last message makes me think I better not keep her waiting any longer.

'It'll just take a second,' I say as I ring her number, but Daryl suddenly snatches my phone from my hand and tosses it behind himself, and I watch it bounce across the grass into the darkness.

'Hey!' I cry, drawing the line at him throwing my expensive phone around so carelessly.

'Just leave it. You're an adult. You don't need to tell your mum where you are all the time,' he says to me, and then he tries to kiss me again, but I'm annoyed with him, so I push him off and get to my feet. I feel bad for doing so, but while I've been tiptoeing around him and trying to keep him in a good mood ever since he got here, I'm not just going to let him treat my things with such disrespect.

At first, I think that I'm not going to be able to find my phone because of how dark it is, but then I see the screen light up several yards away from me. Mum must be calling me again, and I don't mind that because it's helping me locate my device. But as I go over to pick it up, Daryl tells me again to leave it.

Ignoring him, I pick up my phone and answer the call and when I do, I hear Mum's breathless voice at the other end of the line.

'Ellie! Where are you?'

'I'm at the park. What's wrong?'

'Is Daryl with you?'

'Yeah, of course.'

'Listen to me, Ellie. You need to get away from him now.'

'What?'

'Just do as I say. Please, just get away from him.'

I have absolutely no idea why Mum has got herself worked up into such a state, but unless she can give me a good reason why I have to get away from my boyfriend, then I am not going to do as she says. But then she doesn't need to because I hear Daryl tell me to put the phone down, and when I turn around to look at him, I witness him do something that sends a shiver down my spine.

He lifts his t-shirt up and removes a knife that was tucked into the waistline of his jeans.

It's at that moment that I wonder if that was the reason he stopped me earlier when my hands were wandering down his body. He didn't want me to notice what he was hiding under there. But I know all about the knife now, though I have no idea what Daryl plans to do with it.

'What are you doing?' I ask Daryl, with Mum still on the line.

'Put the phone down, Ellie,' Daryl says as he takes a step towards me, but I don't move back because I'm frozen with fear, though I probably should try and move because as the blade catches the moonlight, I realise that dangerous object is only getting closer to me.

'Ellie! What's going on?' Mum asks me. 'Are you okay?'

I hesitate in answering that question because I'm not sure yet but judging by the look in Daryl's eyes, I fear not. Then he speaks again and confirms my nightmare.

'I didn't want to do this to you,' Daryl says quietly and calmly as he takes another step closer. 'Honestly, I told myself that I would leave you alone and not come here. I had a close call back home and thought it would be best if I just stopped before I made things any worse. But I can't, Ellie. I can't stop. I need to do this. I want to do this.'

Daryl starts to raise the knife then, and as he gets ever nearer, I realise he's only a couple of seconds away from being within striking distance. But I'm still stuck to the spot I stand on because as well as being scared, I'm confused.

'What are you talking about?' I ask him. 'What do you mean you can't stop?'

'Oh, Ellie, you don't deserve this. I know that. But neither did Aubree. It's just me. I can't help myself. I feel compelled to do this. I wish I could explain it, but I can't. I'm just so sorry this has to happen.'

The knife is fully raised above Daryl's head now, and that's when my brain forces my body into action, and I turn to run away as fast as I can.

But as Daryl gives chase and I struggle to see where I am going in the darkness, I fear I may already be too late.

40

DAWN

The phone line connecting me to Ellie went dead ten minutes ago, and despite my frantic efforts to speak to her again, she is not picking up. But at least I know she is at the park, and that's where I'm going now, making the short journey in my car and breaking every speed limit on these roads in my desperate attempt to get there before it's too late.

I couldn't hear everything that was being said between Ellie and Daryl when I was on the phone to her, but I could detect fear in my daughter's voice, and I know that something was wrong.

Terrifyingly, it seems that my worst fears might be true, and it's Daryl, rather than his dad, who is actually the dangerous one.

I take another corner far too fast, and as my car's headlights flash across the entrance sign to the park, I speed through the open driveway and down the main path that cuts through this green space. Fortunately, this is not one of those parks that gets locked up at night but while that has made it easy for me to get inside, it also made it easy for Ellie and Daryl to get in here earlier, and I somehow have to try and find them in this large, dark space.

Beeping my car horn, I'm hoping Ellie hears me and comes running towards me. If not, I hope it at least tells her that I am here and help is on the way. But that'll only be the case if she can hear the horn.

What if she can't?

It'll mean I'm already too late to help her.

I have no choice but to slow down because even with my headlights, it's hard to see out here, and I'm worried about hitting something with my car.

As I come to a stop, I leap out from behind the wheel and begin calling my daughter's name as I turn on the torchlight on my phone and shine it all around me. But all I see are bushes and trees, and Ellie could be anywhere in here, her body lying somewhere behind all this lush vegetation, and locating her feels like a completely hopeless cause. But I can't give up, and I continue to shout Ellie's name, desperate to hear her answer me and let me know not only where she is in this park, but also that she is still alright.

But I'm the only one currently making any noise out here, and as I move on, flashing my torch light across the ground in front of me so I can see the way, I catch a glimpse of something truly horrifying.

Blood.

There are drops of it all over the path in front of me, and as I kneel down to get a closer look, I see the blood is also on the grass as well.

My heart is thumping fast while my brain is telling me this proves I am already too late to save her, but I have to force myself to go on, and as I follow the trail of blood, I move between two trees and into denser foliage.

I scratch my arm on a protruding branch and scrape my head on a low hanging one for good measure, but that's only because I'm paying less attention to where I'm going and more on keeping my eyes firmly on the ground for more blood. But then I don't need to follow that red-speckled trail anymore because I get another clue as to where Ellie might be.

I hear her scream.

'Ellie!' I call out as I take off running in the direction of the blood-curdling sound, and as I race forward, I almost lose my footing several times as I stumble over dead tree stumps and get my feet caught in vines a couple of times. But as I hear another scream, I know I'm very close to my daughter, and suddenly, I'm in a clearing in the middle of the park, and I can see two figures up ahead of me.

One of them is Ellie, and she is lying on the ground with her hands up above her head, trying to shield herself from something. The other figure is Daryl, and he is standing over my frightened daughter with a knife in his hand, looking ready to bring it down upon her any second now.

'No!' I cry as I rush towards them both, but while Ellie sees me coming, Daryl does not even bother to turn around and acknowledge my presence here.

He seems entirely focused on finishing the task at hand.

Desperate to get to him before he can do any more harm, I launch my phone in his direction, hoping it might hit him and distract him. But it misses hopelessly, flying off into the bushes behind, and now I've lost my torchlight. Things only seem to get worse when I trip on something heavy and hard, and as I fall to the ground, I fear I have just lost my one and only shot at saving my child.

But then I see what I tripped on. It's a large rock just lying in the middle of this clearing, and before I have even had time to really think about what I'm doing, I have picked it up and am running towards Daryl again.

I see him lunge at Ellie, but she manages to narrowly evade the slashing of the knife, though her attacker is poised to try again already. But I make sure he can't do that because I smash the rock against the back of his head as hard as I can, and the second it makes contact, I already know he won't be recovering from the forceful blow.

The sound of his skull cracking is deafening in this otherwise silent park, and as Daryl collapses to the ground by my feet, I drop the bloodied rock and focus on making sure Ellie is okay.

My first thought is that she is not because I see blood on her hands and arms and fear there may be several deep stab wounds on her body that I haven't even got to yet. But then she tells me that she is okay, that they are just superficial cuts, and as we hug each other tightly, I realise she's not the only one who is okay.

I am too.

That's because I've just saved my daughter's life and, by extension, my own.

41

ELLIE

The bandages currently on my hands and arms are covering the injuries I sustained from my ex-boyfriend, but once they come off, the scars of my last few moments with him will be revealed. But I guess it's the deeper scars that might be more difficult to deal with as my recovery progresses. They are the mental scars that come from knowing I was almost killed by somebody I loved and that I was only saved at the last second by the person sitting by my hospital bed now.

I know it is the psychological scars rather than the superficial ones that Mum is more worried about because she is showing me another website on her phone for yet another therapist whom she thinks it would be a good idea for me to see once I have been discharged from hospital. But I've already told her that it's too early to be thinking about any of that. I just want to rest and recuperate, but because Mum is only trying her best to make sure I'm okay, I let her down gently.

'Can we talk about this tomorrow?' I ask before tentatively reaching out for the cup of water on the table by my bed.

'Here, I've got it,' Mum says, and she holds the cup to my mouth before gently tilting it so the cool liquid slips down my throat and quenches my considerable thirst. I suppose I shouldn't complain about not having full use of my hands yet with all these bandages on because I've lived to tell the tale of my scary night in the park, so I know I am lucky. But it is annoying having to have people doing such simple tasks for me, like helping me eat, drink and go to the toilet.

But things could have been so much worse. While Daryl's knife made contact with me several times during my efforts to fend him off, none of the wounds were mortal. That doesn't mean all the cuts I sustained in the attack aren't painful, though, and as I let out a slight groan before wriggling gingerly in my bed, Mum asks me if I am in need of more painkillers, and I nod my head to confirm that would be good.

I push the call button by my bed that should send a nurse scurrying into this room but there seems to be a delay, so Mum goes to find somebody out in the corridor. As she does that, I let out a sign of frustration because while I've only been in this hospital for forty-eight hours, I already cannot wait to get out of here and go home. I just want things to go back to normal, though it will probably be more like a new version of normal now rather than the one I used to know.

I'm no longer just Ellie Andrews from Suffolk, England. I'm now a survivor of a brutal attack by a psychopathic American, and I very nearly became a statistic of serious crime. Domestic violence. Assault. Murder. Those are all words that can be associated with me now, but I am just trying to focus on the only word that really matters when applied to me.

Alive.

Daryl was successful in fooling me, but he ultimately failed because I am still here, and he is not. He died trying to kill me, so it was nothing less than he deserved, and I won't be shedding any tears for him, that's for sure. I'm angry at him but not just because of what he did to me. It's because of what he did to Aubree as well because she was his first victim, and unlike me, she did not survive her encounter with the dangerous and deadly Californian kid who looked totally innocent on the surface but harboured a terrible bloodlust beneath it.

As Mum returns to the room with a nurse I don't recognise, I prepare to be given more pain medication. I guess I'll have to get used to this because it will be a while before I no longer require drugs to make me feel like myself again.

As the nurse does her job and my pain levels are reduced, I can relax a little more again, and once Mum and I are back to being alone, I decide to talk about something that has been on my mind ever since I was put in this room.

'This is the first time I've been back here since Dad was a patient,' I say quietly, knowing it will also be the first time Mum has been at this hospital since then too.

'Yeah,' she says with a slow nod of her head, and the pair of us have a quiet moment as we each reflect back on that difficult time when we would make daily trips here to see our loved one in his own hospital room, hooked up to all sorts of machines with wires coming out of him and way more nurses and doctors visiting him than I've had so far. But despite his terrible condition and the fact we could see he was getting weaker every time we visited, Dad always kept a positive outlook, and to honour that memory, I know I should do the same myself now.

'Let's go for a walk,' I say to Mum, putting a smile on my face to show her that I feel up to such a thing. 'I want to get some fresh air.'

It takes a little more convincing before Mum agrees that I can go and stretch my legs, and she even checks with a nurse if it is a sensible thing to do, but the nurse has no issues with me getting out of bed for a short time, so I gingerly head out into the corridor with Mum close by my side.

We make our way past various rooms, seeing plenty of patients en route, before we make it to the place I intended us to visit. It's a place I spent some time in before Dad passed away and a place I always told myself I'd come back to one day to commemorate him, though it's proven more difficult since then to pluck up the strength to actually return.

We're in the memorial garden of the hospital, the place where flowers are left by family members to remember those they have lost here, and it's a place I once came to just before Dad slipped away. Back then, I was trying to tell myself that Dad did not belong here and I would never have to be one of those leaving flowers, but now I'm here, I feel like I should have come back a long time ago.

'We should bring flowers here,' I say to Mum as we look around at all the colourful bouquets that have been left by other mourners.

'That would be nice,' Mum agrees as she puts her arm around me and tells me how proud Dad would have been of the woman I have become.

After shedding a few tears and sharing some funny stories about the man we miss so much, Mum and I leave the memorial garden, and I get back into my bed to get some more rest. Despite assuring me that she is not tired and is happy to stay with me for a little while longer, I tell Mum to go home and get some sleep, though she promises me she will be back later tonight when visiting hours start again.

'Can you bring my diary with you when you come back?' I ask her just before she leaves.

'Is that a good idea? I don't think you should be trying to write until your hands have healed!' Mum says sceptically.

'I'm not trying to write,' I reassure her because that's not my plan, 'I just want to read back over it. Then I'm going to get rid of it.'

'Get rid of it?'

'Yeah, it'll help me move on. There's a lot of stuff about Dad and Daryl in there. I'll read it all one more time, and then it's full focus on the future. I've been thinking I'm going to look for an office job so I can work more sociable hours. Then I can see people at night or work on my writing. I might also see if any of my friends want to rent a place with me. A few of them are single again, too, so I think they'll be up for it. I think we could all do with a break from boys for a while.'

'You mean you might actually move out of my house one day?'

'Maybe. But don't get your hopes up just yet.'

We both laugh before Mum tells me she is only joking and that I can stay forever if I want to, and the lovely thing is that I can actually see she means it.

'See you later,' Mum says as she leaves my room, and I give her a wave of one of my bandaged hands before the door closes. Then I relax back onto my pillow, resting my head and feeling grateful for the woman who not only saved my life but has kept me going since Dad went before us both.

She might embarrass, annoy and infuriate me at times, but there is no doubt about it.

Mum loves me.

And I love her too.

42

DAWN

While I can't wait for Ellie to be discharged and be allowed home from the hospital, I know I should take advantage of having the place to myself for a little while yet, so that's what I intend to do. I have put music on, I have poured a glass of wine, a takeaway has been ordered and I'm currently reclining on the sofa with the TV remote in my hand.

The house is quiet.

Peaceful.

Bliss.

It's been three days since the nightmare in the park, and a lot has happened since then, which is why I so desperately need this respite time. My first concern was making sure Ellie was okay, and thankfully, she was, but the police officers who attended the scene had a more pressing concern of their own. They wanted to know exactly what had happened and how a young American man visiting the country had ended up dead.

I can't blame them for interrogating me, both at the hospital and at the police station the following day. I understand why they had so many questions for me, and I also understand why they couldn't just take my word for it and believe what I was telling them. They wouldn't have been doing their job if they hadn't been sceptical and assessed all the evidence before making up their mind that I had merely been acting in defence of my daughter and that Daryl had died because he was trying to kill her.

The evidence itself was pretty conclusive because not only did mine and Ellie's stories match, but there was plenty of proof of how dangerous Daryl had been due to the fact that Ellie had sustained multiple injuries and her blood was all over the park. The injuries were consistent with a knife wound, and seeing as how only Daryl's fingerprints were on the weapon that was found by his body, it was obvious he had been the only one using it.

The knife itself had been taken from my kitchen, and Ellie believes he must have secretly taken it when he had left her bedroom to go to the toilet shortly before he suggested they go out to watch the sunset. It was a knife I recognised, although not one I had used for a very long time because there hadn't been much cooking going on with all the microwave meals I have been sustaining myself on lately. But with that weapon examined, the scene assessed by forensic experts and mine and Ellie's stories painstakingly corroborated, the police decided that what we had told them was the truth, and I was free to go.

So how does it feel to get away with murder?

I don't see it as murder at all.

I see it as merely me doing what any mother would have done in that situation.

I would die for my daughter, but I would also kill for her, and while I never expected to actually have to do such a drastic thing, I didn't hesitate to do so when the moment called for it.

But despite my best attempts to do nothing but chill out this evening, I find it impossible to do something I probably shouldn't, and before I know it, I'm back on the American news website that streams its coverage online. My reason for doing so is because I want to see what is being said about Daryl over there because while I know the media here has been full of reports of the attack in the park and how I saved my daughter from the deadly clutches of a crazy Californian, I haven't had much time to check the news overseas.

I start the streaming and sit back, taking a sip of my wine as I listen to the reporter on screen talking about a possible hurricane that is headed for Florida. But then they move on to the next story and when they do, I see the face of the young man I was forced to kill.
Unsurprisingly, the death of an American overseas in such dramatic circumstances has hit the headlines, but even more so because of the deceased's connection with another man who has only recently started serving a sentence for a heinous crime too. Daryl's dad was already newsworthy, so now Daryl has joined him, they have certainly given the journalists over there plenty to work with.

But as I watch the latest report, I get confirmation of a thing I already suspected on the night I saved Ellie's life. Harvey has admitted to the police that he lied about being Aubree's killer and confessed that he was trying to deflect attention from his son, the real killer. He has spoken about how he found out what Daryl had done to Aubree after his son had anxiously told him

as the police were standing at their front door, waiting to come inside after my earlier tip-off.
With the knowledge of his son's crimes and the location of the body, Harvey was able to pervert the course of justice, which carries a lengthy prison sentence of its own, but it's one that has a much shorter timeframe attached to it than the crime he was already behind bars for.

Ellie has told the police here that Daryl confessed his killing of Aubree to her just before he attacked her in the park, and that was quickly passed on to the authorities in America, resulting in this rather dramatic turn of events that is now keeping U.S. viewers glued to the news with great interest. It's a mad story to think that Harvey would do something so drastic to keep his son out of trouble, but because any parent might be able to sympathise with that, I'm sure there are more than a few people watching this news coverage now and feeling a little sorry for Harvey.

And believe it or not, I am one of them.

Yes, his actions made it harder in the long run for Aubree's family to get to the real truth, and yes, him allowing Daryl to stay on the outside almost resulted in Ellie's demise, things I and most other people could never forgive him for. But I also understand the place he was in and where his head was at when he must have made that huge decision to confess to a crime he didn't actually commit. I can also look at the situation he is left in now, with both his wife and son dead, and try to imagine the world of pain he must be living in while he still resides in a prison cell.

He's lost everything, so what is keeping him going at this point?

I can't think of anything.

Then again, there is one word that crosses my mind, though I try to push it away quickly because it's a scary one.

Revenge.

Harvey must hate me for what I did to Daryl. I killed his only child to save mine, and while I was justified in doing so, does he see it that way? Will he also have figured out that I was the one who tipped off the police and started the process that resulted in him having to make a false confession just to keep his son out of prison? I'd say so based on how quickly we left and how soon after that the police showed up at the door and searched the basement for the photo.

If I had to guess, I'd say Harvey had no idea that photo was down there and that it was Daryl who had printed it off at some point, most likely as a sick souvenir to remember his victim by. But that photo ended up being the thing that brought this whole thing crashing down on his head, quite literally in the case of the weapon I used to kill him.

So how is Harvey feeling towards me? I feel unsettled not knowing the answer, and even though he is currently in police custody thousands of miles away, he won't be in there forever, not now his charges have been downgraded. He'll be out much sooner than he should have been and when he is, what will he do next?

I consider the idea of writing him a letter, one in which I explain to him, in my own words, exactly what happened so that he understands it all from my point of view. Parent to parent. Maybe that will work, and after all, we were friends at one point in time. I could tell him that I understand why he did what he did to protect Daryl, but he also has to understand why I was forced to do what I did to protect Ellie.

Should I do that?

Should I try and make contact with him?

Or should I just let sleeping dogs lie?

I have a funny feeling I'm going to spend an awfully long time trying to make that choice, and only time will tell if it proves to be the right one.

EPILOGUE

HARVEY

Being confined to a 6ft by 8ft cell for the next two years of my life means I am going to have a lot of time to do a lot of thinking, and that's pretty much all I can do as I lie on my uncomfortable mattress and stare at the bars that cover most of my window.

Prison is not a place for those who can't be comfortable with their own thoughts because thoughts are all a person really has in here. All my freedoms and liberties have been stripped from me since I became a prisoner with a number on the back of my uniform, and now I'm just a body who is told when to eat, sleep and work. The only pleasure in my day comes from thinking about the world on the outside: the wide open spaces, the green grass and the golden sands, the blue skies and the palm trees, and the ability for a person to go where they want when they want.

All those things feel a million miles away from where I am currently, but I know I will be out one day. Until then, I just have to let the clock run down.

'Mail!'

The unexpected cry from the prison warden outside my door surprises me, and as I look at the piece of paper that has just been dropped into my cell, I have absolutely no idea what it could be about. I don't get mail that frequently here, but then again, that is to be expected when I'm one of the most hated men in the country for lying about what happened to Aubree and putting her family through even more pain than they had already been through, so who would rush to be pen pals with a dangerous man like me?

Saying that, the few letters I have received since being in here have come from women who could be considered dangerous themselves because they are the type who seem to gravitate towards bad men who have done bad things and are now kept under lock and key for the considerable future. I've had invitations in the post here to begin relationships with women from Alabama and Kentucky, and there was even a marriage proposal from an elderly lady in Seattle who told me she heard about my story on the news and felt compelled to reach out to me and offer me hope.

Yep, *crazy.*

As I pick up the letter on the floor, I wonder if it will be yet another one of those strange fans I seem to have acquired since I became famous and if it is, at least I will get five minutes of mild entertainment before I screw the paper up and toss it back onto the floor. But when I start reading this latest letter, I realise that it has not been written by some lonely woman looking for an isolated criminal to love. It has been written by a woman I knew in the outside world before I landed in here.

It's a letter from Dawn.

I read it through word for word twice before I put it back down but when I do, I don't screw it up like I expected to. I gently rest it on my bed because I already know it's something I'm going to read again, most likely many times while I am in here.

Walking over to the window, I scratch the stubble on my chin and think about how I never expected Ellie's mum to get in touch with me, though I am quite glad that she has now that she's reached out. In her letter, she has tried to explain to me why she had no choice but to kill Daryl, and she has also said that just like me, she was doing whatever she could to protect her child. I guess this is her way of apologising for taking my son's life and alleviating some of the guilt she might feel about me having lost another member of my family, making me the sole survivor.

I know Dawn didn't have to do this. She could have just got on with her life and forgotten all about me, focussing on her future happiness as well as Ellie's. I imagine they both have a lot to live for and a lot to look forward to, which is more than can be said for me. But Dawn has misread me, and despite what she might think about me languishing away in this cell with nobody waiting for me on the outside, she would be wrong, at least in the sense of one thing.

I do have something to look forward to.

I look forward to getting my revenge on her and her daughter.

Letting out a deep sigh as I return to my mattress and lie down again, hearing the old springs creaking below me as I get into position, I consider how despite everything, I have got lucky in one sense. The police know about my recent crimes in terms of misleading their investigation into Aubree's death and how I tried to protect the real killer so he could continue to walk free, but they have no idea about the one in my distant past.

The one in which I killed my wife, Daryl's mother, and made it look like an accident.

The coroner recorded Jodie's cause of death as a heart attack, and while that is technically what killed her, it's the thing that brought on the heart attack that only I am aware of.

Aconite poisoning. That's how I killed my wife and got away with it, using the "Queen of Poisons" to kill the queen of my family, and it was easy to do. Aconite is a plant, but while it looks pretty when in full bloom, it can be harmful if it comes into contact with humans, particularly if absorbed through the skin. That meant Jodie was doomed the moment I secretly added aconite into her skin cream, and after she had applied it, the poison did its work on her body within four hours, causing heart failure. I knew the doctors wouldn't go looking for poison in her bloodstream but just to be sure, I safely disposed of the bottle of skin cream so they wouldn't find it at the house and figure out what I had done.

It felt good to take a life, not just because I had felt myself drifting apart from Jodie over the years, but because I'd always had a morbid fascination with death, and particularly murder, compelled to try it one day and know what it would feel like. They say the apple doesn't fall far from the tree, and that can certainly be said about me and my son. He has the same deadly tendencies towards women as I do, although unlike him, I was mostly able to control mine, barring my one deadly act, and I did a good job of getting away with it. But Daryl was far more impulsive than I was and didn't really think things through, evident in how he attacked Ellie in the UK when he must have known he had no way of getting away with it. But I am more measured than him, and despite wanting to hurt lots of people in my time, I have only ever hurt one.

The woman I married.

I killed Jodie after growing tired of our relationship but not wanting to go through the messy and expensive process of a divorce, one that would have most likely seen me have to move out of our lovely home and start again elsewhere. Of course, I felt bad for leaving Daryl motherless, and he never knew that I was the reason his mum died, but I couldn't help myself. I had to do it, and I did, just like Daryl ended up killing Aubree and almost Ellie too. There is a deadly streak in the men in this family, and I wonder if my male ancestors were bloodthirsty men who took lives easily back in the old Wild West days. Maybe that's where I get it from, and maybe that's the terrible gene that was passed down to Daryl too. Whatever the cause of it, we're both killers.

But unlike my son, I am not done yet.

It's going to take a while, but I will be allowed out of here one day and when I am, there are a couple of people I want to pay a visit to, namely Dawn and Ellie in England, and when I get there, I want to surprise them.

They must pay for what they have done, and they will.

I will see to that.

In the meantime, I will reread Dawn's letter and have a good chuckle at how she has written it from a position in which she assumes she has come out of all this in a better place than me. Of course she hasn't. She is not as clever as she thinks she is.

She should be more careful.

I'm just as dangerous as her daughter's boyfriend was.

And one day, I just might prove it to her.

Or at least die trying.

THE END

Download My Free Book

If you would like to receive a FREE copy of my psychological thriller 'Just One Second', then you can find the link to the book at my website www.danielhurstbooks.com

Thank you for reading *My Daughter's Boyfriend.*

If you have enjoyed this psychological thriller, then you'll be pleased to know that I have several more stories in this genre, and you can find a list of my titles on the next page. These include my most popular book *Til Death Do Us Part*, which has a twist that very few people have been able to predict, and *The Doctor's Wife*, which became the #1 selling book in the UK Kindle Store in February 2023.

ALSO BY DANIEL HURST

TIL DEATH DO US PART
THE PASSENGER
WE USED TO LIVE HERE
THE DOCTOR'S WIFE
THE INTRUDER
WHAT MY FAMILY SAW
THE HOLIDAY HOME
THE BRIDE TO BE
HER LAST HOUR
RUN AWAY WITH ME
THE RIVALS
WE TELL NO ONE
THE WOMAN AT THE DOOR
HE WAS A LIAR
THE BROKEN VOWS
THE WRONG WOMAN
NO TIME TO BE ALONE
THE TUTOR
THE NEIGHBOURS
THE BREAK
THE ROLE MODEL
THE BOYFRIEND
THE PROMOTION
THE NEW FRIENDS
THE ACCIDENT

(All books available now on Amazon and Kindle Unlimited – read on to learn a little more about selected titles...)

TIL DEATH DO US PART

What if your husband was your worst enemy?

Megan thinks that she has the perfect husband and the perfect life. Craig works all day so that she doesn't have to, leaving her free to relax in their beautiful and secluded country home. But when she starts to long for friends and purpose again, Megan applies for a job in London, much to her husband's disappointment. She thinks he is upset because she is unhappy. But she has no idea.

When Megan secretly attends an interview and meets a recruiter for a drink, Craig decides it is time to act. Locking her away in their home, Megan realises that her husband never had her best interests at heart. Worse, they didn't meet by accident. Craig has been planning it all from the start.

As Megan is kept shut away from the world with only somebody else's diary for company, she starts to uncover the lies, the secrets, and the fact that she isn't actually Craig's first wife after all...

THE PASSENGER

She takes the same train every day. But this is a journey she will never forget…

Amanda is a hardworking single mum, focused on her job and her daughter, Louise. But it's also time she did something for herself, and after saving for years, she is now close to quitting her dreary 9-5 and following her dream.

But then, on her usual commute home from London to Brighton, she meets a charming stranger – a man who seems to know everything about her. Then he delivers an ultimatum. She needs to give him the code to her safe where she keeps her savings before they reach Brighton – or she will never see Louise again.

Amanda is horrified, but while she knows the threat is real, she can't give him the code. That's because the safe contains something other than her money. It holds a secret. *A secret so terrible it will destroy both her's and her daughter's life if it ever gets out...*

THE WRONG WOMAN

What if you were the perfect person to get revenge?

Simone used to be the woman other women would use if they suspected their partner was cheating. She would investigate, find out the truth and if the men were guilty, exact revenge in one form or another. But after things went wrong with one particular couple, Simone was forced to go into hiding to evade the law.

Having assumed a new identity, Simone is now Mary, a mild-mannered woman who doesn't raise her voice or get angry, meaning nobody would ever suspect her of being capable of the things she used to do for a living. But when she finds out that her new boyfriend is having an affair, it awakens in her the person she used to be. Plotting revenge, Mary reverts back to the woman she once was before she went on the run and became domesticated. That means Simone is back, and it also means that her boyfriend and his mistress are in for the shock of their lives.

They messed with her. *But they picked the wrong woman.*

THE WOMAN AT THE DOOR

It was a perfect Saturday night. *Until she knocked on the door...*

Rebecca and Sam are happily married and enjoying a typical Saturday night until a knock at the door changes everything. There's a woman outside, and she has something to say. Something that will change the happy couple's relationship forever...

With their marriage thrown into turmoil, Rebecca no longer knows who to trust, while Sam is determined to find out who that woman was and why she came to their house. But the problem is that he doesn't know who she is and why she has targeted them.

Desperate to save his marriage, Sam is willing to do anything to find the truth, even if it means breaking the law. But as time goes by and things only seem to get worse, it looks like he could lose Rebecca forever.

THE NEIGHBOURS

It seemed like the perfect house on the perfect street. *Until they met the neighbours...*

Happily married couple, Katie and Sean, have plenty to look forward to as they move into their new home and plan for the future. But then they meet two of their new neighbours, and everything on their quiet street suddenly doesn't seem as desirable as it did before.

Having been warned about the other neighbours and their adulterous and criminal ways, Katie and Sean realise that they are going to have to be on their guard if they want to make their time here a happy one.

But some of the other neighbours seem so nice, and that's why they choose to ignore the warning and get friendly with the rest of the people on the street. *And that is why their marriage will never be the same again...*

THE TUTOR

What if you invited danger into your home?

Amy is a loving wife and mother to her husband, Nick, and her two children, Michael and Bella. It's that dedication to her family that causes her to seek help for her teenage son when it becomes apparent that he is going to fail his end of school exams.

Enlisting the help of a professional tutor, Amy is certain that she is doing the best thing for her son and, indeed, her family. But when she discovers that there is more to this tutor than meets the eye, it is already too late.

With the rest of her family enamoured by the tutor, Amy is the only one who can see that there is something not quite right about her. But as the tutor becomes more involved in Amy's family, it's not just the present that is threatened. Secrets from the past are exposed too, and by the time everything is out in the open, Amy isn't just worried about her son and his exams anymore. She is worried for the survival of her entire family.

HE WAS A LIAR

What if you never really knew the man you loved?

Sarah is in a loving relationship with Paul, a seemingly perfect man who she is hoping to marry and start a family with one day, until his sudden death sends her into a world of pain.

Trying to come to terms with her loss, Sarah finds comfort in going through some of Paul's old things, including his laptop and his emails. But after finding something troubling, Sarah begins to learn things about Paul that she never knew before, and it turns out he wasn't as perfect as she thought. But as she unravels more about his secretive past, she ends up not only learning things that break her heart, but things that the police will be interested to know too.

Sarah can't believe what she has discovered. But it's only when she keeps digging that she realises it's not just her late boyfriend's secrets that are contained on the laptop. Other people's secrets are too, and they aren't dead, which means they will do anything to protect them.

RUN AWAY WITH ME

What if your partner was wanted by the police?

Laura is feeling content with her life. She is married, she has a good home, and she is due to give birth to her first child any day now. But her perfect world is shattered when her husband comes home flustered and afraid. He's made a terrible mistake. He's done a bad thing. *And now the police are going to be looking for him.*

There's only one way out of this. He wants to run. *But he won't go without his wife...*

Laura knows it is wrong. She knows they should stay and face the music. But she doesn't want to lose her man. She can't raise this baby alone. *So she agrees to go with him.* But life on the run is stressful and unpredictable, and as time goes by, Laura worries she has made a terrible mistake. They should never have ran. But it's too late for that now. Her life is ruined. The only question is: *how will it end?*

THE ROLE MODEL

She raised her. Now she must help her…

Heather is a single mum who has always done what's best for her daughter, Chloe. From childhood up to the age of seventeen, Chloe has been no trouble. That is until one night when she calls her mother with some shocking news. There's been an accident. *And now there's a dead body…*

As always, Heather puts her daughter's safety before all else, but this might be one time when she goes too far. Instead of calling the emergency services, Heather hides the body, saving her daughter from police interviews and public outcry.

But as she well knows, everything she does has an impact on her child's behaviour, and as time goes on and the pair struggle to keep their sordid secret hidden, Heather begins to think that she hasn't been such a good mum after all. *In fact, she might have been the worst role model ever…*

THE BROKEN VOWS

He broke his word to her. Now she wants revenge…

Alison is happily married to Graham, or at least she is until she finds out that he has been cheating on her. Graham has broken the vows he made on his wedding day. How could he do it? It takes Alison a while to figure it out, but at least she has time on her side. *Only that is where she is wrong.*

A devastating diagnosis means the clock is ticking down on her life now, and if she wants revenge on her cheating partner, then she is going to have to act fast. Alison does just that, implementing a dangerous and deadly plan, and it's one that will have far reaching consequences for several people, including her clueless husband.

WE USED TO LIVE HERE

How much do you know about your house?

When the Burgess family move into their 'forever' home, it seems like they are set for many happy years together at their new address. Steph and Grant, along with their two children, Charlie and Amelia, settle into their new surroundings quickly. But then they receive a visit from a couple who claim to have lived in their house before and wish to have a look around for old time's sake. They seem pleasant and plausible, so Steph invites them in. And that's when things start to change…

It's not long after the peculiar visit when the homeowners start to find evidence of the past all around their new home as they redecorate. But it's the discovery of a hidden wall containing several troubling messages that really sends Steph into a spin, and after digging deeper into the history of the house a little more, she learns it is connected to a shocking crime from the past. *A crime that still remains unsolved...*

Every house has secrets. But some don't stay buried forever…

THE 20 MINUTES SERIES

What readers are saying:

"If you like people watching, then you will love these books!"

"The psychological insight was fascinating, the stories were absorbing and the characters were 3D. I absolutely loved it."

"The books in this series are an incredibly easy read, you become invested in the lives of the characters so easily, and I am eager to know more and more. Roll on the next book."

THE 20 MINUTES SERIES (in order)

20 MINUTES ON THE TUBE
20 MINUTES LATER
20 MINUTES IN THE PARK
20 MINUTES ON HOLIDAY
20 MINUTES BY THE THAMES
20 MINUTES AT HALLOWEEN
20 MINUTES AROUND THE BONFIRE
20 MINUTES BEFORE CHRISTMAS
20 MINUTES OF VALENTINE'S DAY
20 MINUTES TO CHANGE A LIFE
20 MINUTES IN LAS VEGAS
20 MINUTES IN THE DESERT

20 MINUTES ON THE ROAD
20 MINUTES BEFORE THE WEDDING
20 MINUTES IN COURT
20 MINUTES BEHIND BARS
20 MINUTES TO MIDNIGHT
20 MINUTES BEFORE TAKE OFF
20 MINUTES IN THE AIR
20 MINUTES UNTIL IT'S OVER

About The Author

Daniel Hurst lives in the Northwest of England with his wife, Harriet, and daughter, Penny, and if that doesn't make him lucky enough, he considers himself extremely fortunate to be able to write stories every day for his readers.

You can visit him at his online home www.danielhurstbooks.com

You can connect with Daniel on Facebook at www.facebook.com/danielhurstbooks or on Instagram at www.instagram.com/danielhurstbooks

He is always happy to receive emails from readers at daniel@danielhurstbooks.com and replies to every single one.

Thank you for reading.

Daniel

MY DAUGHTER'S BOYFRIEND by Daniel Hurst published by Daniel Hurst Books Limited, The Coach House, 31 View Road, Rainhill, Merseyside, L35 0LF

Front Cover Design by 100Covers

Printed in Great Britain
by Amazon

23604761R00169